I0418197

ILLUMINE
BOOK ONE IN THE ILLUMINE SERIES

ILLUMINE

BOOK ONE IN THE ILLUMINE SERIES

ILLUMINE

BOOK ONE IN THE ILLUMINE SERIES

ALIVIA ANDERS

RED ALICE PRESS

This book is a work of fiction. Any reference to historical events and real people are used fictitiously. Other names, characters, places, and events are product of the author's imagination, and any resemblance to living people is entirely coincidental.

ILLUMINE
ISBN 978-0-9911-9473-5

The publisher acknowledges the copyright holder of the individual works as follows:

ILLUMINE
Copyright © 2012 by Alivia Anders

OBUMBRATE
Copyright © 2012 by Alivia Anders

A SHARD OF ICE
Copyright © 2013 by Alivia Anders

AN ICE PRINCESS HEART: A SHARD OF ICE NOVELLA
Copyright © 2013 by Alivia Anders

All rights reserved. No portion of this work may be copied, transmitted, or stored, electronically or otherwise without the written consent of the author, except for use in review.

Cover design: Regina Wamba
Interior design: White Rabbit Designs
Interior formatting: White Rabbit Designs

Red Alice Press
www.redalicepress.com
Logo design: Kathryn Quinn

Manufactured in the United States of America

If you have purchased this book without a cover, please be aware that this book is "stripped" and the author has garnered no royalties from it.

Other books by Alivia Anders

The Illumine Series
Illumine
Obumbrate
Riven
Ethereal
Alacrity

A Shard of Ice Novellas
An Ice Princess Heart
An Ice Princess Kiss
An Ice Princess Symphony
An Ice Princess Dream

The Black Symphony Saga
A Shard of Ice
A Brush of Fire
A Breath of Life

The Dream Chronicles
Lucid Echelon

ILLUMINE

| BOOK ONE IN THE ILLUMINE SERIES |

ONE
THIS IS YOUR END

They say you have epiphanies in the strangest places.

It isn't something you plan in the morning while you skim over the *Times*, venti soy skinny latte in one hand and a pen in the other. Just as it wasn't something I had planned to have in the middle of a shopping trip with one of New York's youngest socialites, Cassandra Knight.

Standing outside her dressing room doors, my eyes lingered on my cell phone. Tonight was supposed to be the best day of our lives, or so Cassie had proclaimed when she woke me up with her incessant texting at the crack of dawn. We were attending a gallery opening by the infamous Cassius 'Chase' DeRapport, a rising star in all things painted and artistic, and attendance had been declared a must if we wanted to hold onto our golden rings of socialite power.

Only problem was, that nagging little epiphany that struck me three minutes ago, told me the last place I was supposed to be was that party.

The dressing room door flung open, and Cassie strutted out to making a bee-line for the floor-to-ceiling mirrors at the end of the room. She was the kind of drop-dead gorgeous girl every person envied in one way or another, be it for the way every article of clothing seemed perfectly tailored to her lithe frame or the impeccable raw beauty she had inherited from blessed genetics. I watched her with mild interest, sneaking glances at my phone impatiently as she dabbled in front of the mirrors, clearly unsatisfied.

"Essie, hand me the other dress," Cassie groaned, holding out a hand. Her free one ran through the long, straight silky black hair cascading down her back. When I hadn't moved, she quickly added a huffed, "Please."

Grabbing the only other untouched dress from her dressing room, I joined her down the hall, passing her the heavy gown. It was a floor length strapless dress, covered in a hypnotizing sequined pattern of blues and purples, trimmed in the most delicate wisps of lace at the sleeves and hem line. It screamed of something timeless and eye-catching, and inwardly I knew it would be Cassie's way of trying to be one of the pieces of art on display. A petty attempt at drawing attention to herself, but one that worked without fail every time.

She turned around to face me, holding the captivating gown at her side so I could see the one she was wearing- an equally stunning gown in a rich navy and plunging neckline - beside the one that I secretly wished I could own. Her immaculate face frowned. "Help me pick one out. Which one should I get?"

I bit on the tip of my tongue, forcing myself to act mildly interested in the gowns before asking the obvious. "That depends. Are you trying to show-off the fact you have no chest to speak of, or are you aiming to look like one of Chase's finished pieces?"

Caramel colored eyes bored into mine. I would have thought she was annoyed had it not been for the quick flash of a smirk on her petal pink lips.

"Tut-tut," she chided, looking back to the mirror over her shoulder. Her eyes studied the dress meticulously. "Such jealousy, Essallie. I think I see your skin turning green."

I found myself rolling my eyes before I could hold back. "I'm sorry, my Queen. Please, allow me to make it up to you by bowing and kissing your rotten feet."

Finally, Cassie smiled. She fought back a laugh, looking back to me with a much softer gaze. "Why aren't you trying anything on?" She asked, not for the first time today. "Do you already have something for tonight?"

Giving her my best non-committal shrug, I made a noise that sounded like a yes. The change in her eyes from gentle to sharp happened so fast, I felt my skin shiver. Obviously, she didn't buy the bluff.

"Liar," she accused. Cassie regarded me, complete disbelief written on her face as she scowled and stalked back into her dressing room. The door slammed with a clang of metal and wood, Cassie continuing to talk from inside the little box. "This isn't just any party, honestly Essallie. It's your boyfriend's opening gala night. You have to show up in a stunning gown or it'll give everyone the wrong impression."

She didn't have to tell me; having spent the last decade and change in New York City, I knew all too well what *responsibilities* came with being in the center circles of the wealthy and privileged. I was raised by my grandparents, a pair of old-money socialites with a taste for the lavish and exceptional things in life. Had I been here my whole life, it might have felt natural to pay a week's salary on one pair of designer jeans, but the only reason I was in New York at all was due to my mother's failure to thrive. Before I had moved to the Big Apple, I had lived in a cozy old Victorian in Maine and spent my nights hiding through the house with my brother.

If mom hadn't gone off the deep end and landed herself in an institution, I would have still had my cozy home and loving brother. Instead, all I had now were objects to fill the silence of my grandparents' disinterest in me as a person. It was one thing to provide things, it was another to provide love.

Cassie had slipped back into her runway ensemble of black skinny jeans and violet crop top, and was out by my side, sequined dress in hand. She took one look at me before shaking her head. "What is with you today?"

I stared at her, eyes wide. "Nothing."

"Ugh, I hate calling you a liar twice in one day," she scowled again. "Have the past twelve years taught you nothing? They don't call it a sixth sense for nothing, you know."

Of course she knew something was off. It was written all over my face no matter how hard I tried to hide it. Cassie's 'sixth sense' went beyond reading faces and body language, however. One look at someone, and she could tell you exactly what you were thinking, like the mind-reading powers straight out of a teen fiction novel. At first, she had chalked it up to dumb luck. Now she used it like a shield and sword all-in-one combo, picking on random kids in our grade and digging into their thoughts.

I followed Cassie out of the dressing room and watched as she, in her typical indecisiveness, bought both dresses. She barely missed a beat between hearing the total and swiping her Dad's pretty little gold card. I still couldn't believe that had been his gift to Cassie for not skipping classes more than twice a week. Apparently, money talked more than I would ever care to understand.

Nestled into the back of her family's town car, Cassie gave directions to her driver before spreading out on the black leather seats, appearing exhausted. In the right light, her tanned skin showed faint traces of lines and dark spots, even small half-moons under her eyes from sleepless nights out on the town. It was one of the few times she looked normal, not like the ageless, perfect girl I'd stood beside for so many years.

One of Cassie's eyes popped open, and promptly squinted. "Alright, spill the beans, Barbie," she practically commanded. A hand reached out, weaving fingertips through my own long, platinum blonde locks hanging over my shoulders. "Why are you so down in the dumps?"

I had already lied twice, and both times had left me feeling like a shallow shell of a friend. No time like the present to say what was on my mind, not like she wouldn't be able to guess what I was thinking anyway.

"Can't we just... skip the party, Cassie?" I played with the hem of my off-white blouse, twisting my fingers in and out of the fabric. "I bet no one would even notice if we didn't show." We were, in way, Chase's entourage, a pair of groupies and expendable by default. The countless stuck up people who would come out to stare at his work would no doubt be more worried about finding the free wine than two girls.

Cassie studied me for a moment before moving herself up to sit. The glare she gave me sank into my skin, and I felt my face burn.

"Of *course* we can skip it," she said, each bitter word coated in a layer of fake sympathy. "No one would *possibly* notice the artist's girlfriend missing from his party. What was I thinking? We should just stay inside, and cower under the covers like frightened little children." Her words made me flinch, even more so when she laughed and rolled her eyes. "You really need to chill out, Essallie. Why are you trying to scramble out at the last minute like this?"

I opened my mouth to speak, only to close it. My excuse was petty, even I knew that, and there would be no way in convincing Cassie that it would be best to stay home because of some gut feeling that told me to run for the hills. She would tell me it had to be cold feet, that I was reluctant to take the next step in my relationship with Chase.

It was so much more than that, though; things with Chase were... bizarre. I had met him through Cassie at one of her wild summer parties nearly two years ago, and we'd found common ground in the love to draw and express our feelings in artwork. One afternoon he asked me on a date, and it all fell so perfectly into place I never questioned it. But the truth was, I knew almost nothing about the guy I was calling my boyfriend for nearly three months. He was aloof, distant, and a touch unpredictable. At first, the mystery had been enticing, and I had loved dating someone with virtually no strings. But now, it felt off, like I was missing some big puzzle piece of who he was.

Tie in the sudden burst of clarity I had experienced, and I was ready to call it a day.

Glancing nervously at Cassie, I felt my shoulders slump. "I don't know why, honestly. There's this nagging feeling, a bad one-"

"You and your feelings," she muttered, but softened a bit when she saw the torn look on my face. Cassie sighed. "I get it. You're freaking out, but I can promise you, there is nothing to worry about. You're going to go the party, you're going to have a great time laughing at all the awful jokes those stuffy snobs repeat like bad broken records, and then you'll go home. See, not so scary, huh?"

I sat back into my spot, silent. Maybe she was right; maybe I was looking for any excuse to avoid putting myself out there. I may have managed to weave through the higher crowd at school for the last couple of years, but it had never been for my shining personality. Had it not been for Cassie thrusting me into every spotlight, I probably would have spent the better part of my life hiding under the covers, just like she said.

The car came to a stop, and I quickly glanced over to Cassie before muttering a goodbye and stepping out. I had barely shut the door when the window rolled down, and Cassie stuck out her upper half, strands of black hair swinging over her shoulders.

"Essie," she called out, waving a hand at me. Reluctantly, I walked back over to the car, ready to hear some little snarky jab from my best friend, the kind that normally would egg me on and light a fire in my spirits. Instead, she was anything but snarky.

Hands in my pockets, I raised an eyebrow and waited. "Cassandra?"

She made a face, hating to hear her full name, but ignored it. "Look, I'm not supposed to be telling you this." A nervous look crossed her face, and she nibbled on the corner of her bottom lip. "Chase made me promise, but I can't have you not show and-"

"What is it?" I found myself asking, the smallest flare of panic sparking to life in my chest. "What did you promise Chase?"

She wrestled with herself for all of two seconds before letting out a sneer that would curdle dairy, and cursed. "Chase has a surprise for you, okay? Something big planned, some kind of romantic crap." She shook her head at my opened mouth. "No, he didn't give me details. But I'm telling you, if you don't show, you will do so much more than just be a flake. You'll break his damn heart." As quickly as she professed the secret, Cassie's face changed, the self-assured air about her back in place. She flashed me a wicked grin. "So please, wear something nice, and don't screw this up."

Unfortunately, I wasn't.

By the time I had finished getting dressed, minor details and all, I was already running late. Toss in one confused taxi-driver and traffic, and I knew tonight was going to have cringe-worthy written all over it. I stepped out of the taxi, handed over far more than the short ride was worth, and practically ran for the elevator.

For his 'dramatic unveiling', he had insisted on using a half-abandoned building just outside the heart of the city, and had practically demanded it be on the eighth floor. Watching the small panel turn green and flash the number eight, I couldn't help but grin as I made my way down the hall. Chase had even gone as far as to decorate the hallway to set the mood for his event, dimming the lights and adding small pockets of dry ice to create a smoking effect. It was brilliant.

Reaching the entrance, I went to go on in, when I was stopped at the door by a burly looking guy swathed in black.

"No phones allowed inside," he said, tipping a bucket toward me. Inside, several dozen cellphones stared at me, each one tagged with a name scribbled on paper. "Drop the phone, or don't go in."

Normally, I would have baffled at the idea of leaving my phone behind- it was my lifeline. The only thing I had to keep me company if I was stuck in an awkward situation, or a way I could text awful things to Cassie without having to say them aloud. But, it was for Chase, and I had already blown too much time just getting here.

I thrusted him my entire wristlet, walking past him and embracing the loud music that grew with each step inside. "Name's Essallie Hanley."

"How the heck do you spell that?"

"Figure it out," I shouted back, uncaring.

Turning a corner, I was hit full-force with the atmosphere of the party. Sharp, pulsing music thrummed deep in my bones, so loud I could barely think straight. Tiny pockets of white and red light shined like beacons, guiding a pathway to each item on display. People stood in clusters, some hovering near the sparse light sources, others mingling in the near-dark and cradling glasses of wine like newborns.

I spotted Cassie lingering beside the centerpiece of the main room, a stone angel missing its head, dressed in a flowing toga-esque gown and holding a sword made of what looked like red onyx. She waved at me instantly, and pulled me as close as possible when I came over.

"Well?" She half-screamed in my ear. I could hear the excitement bubbling over. "Still scared?"

Staring back at her, I shook my head. She passed me a glass of something that looked like red wine, and nodded up at the statue. "It's interesting stuff, no? Sort of... mysterious."

"More like macabre," I replied. Chase had titled his collection 'Angels on High' but I hadn't thought that he would be actually depicting angels, headless or otherwise. The statue in front of us stood nearly nine feet tall, the top of its jagged, headless neck barely missing the ceiling. I had no idea where Chase could get that much stone, let alone carve the sculpture out. I tilted my head to the side, studying it. Something about the statue tickled the back of my brain, as if I'd seen it somewhere before.

Glancing at Cassie, I pointed at the statue. "Did he tell you what he was working on?"

"Nope, not so much as a single hint," Cassie said with a shrug, but her eyes said otherwise. She looked away from my probing stare. "All he said was something about finally finding the right inspiration."

Huh, because that didn't tip me off or anything. Chase had started preparing his grand unveiling not too long after we started dating, there was an angel theme all about, and Cassie said he had something romantic planned? Crud, he was going to pull out all the stops.

I handed Cassie my untouched wine. "I have to leave."

"Wait, what?" She practically fell over her three-inch heels, running over to stop me from exiting. "You can't go."

"I can't, or you won't let me?"

"Both."

"Cassie," I groaned, and put my hands on her bare shoulders. Her skin burned with heat, and I wondered if she had stood under the lights for too long. "Look, I get it. You're Chase's friend, so you feel like you have some kind of moral obligation to keep us together. But I can't be the center of someone's world like..." I waived one hand around impatiently, "like this. It's just too much."

The hurt and dejected look she gave me far surpassed the anger and attitude I had expected from her. Cassie downed my glass of wine in a single shot, squaring her shoulders. "What do I tell him?"

I sighed. Was I really going to be the girl who broke up with her boyfriend through the mutual friend? No way, even I wasn't that low and shallow. "I'll tell him—"

Fingers laced around my upper arm, another hand wrapping tenderly around my waist. Body heat caressed my back through my dress as lips kissed the side of my neck, slowly moving up to my ear. Chase's voice, all velvet and warm honey, surrounded me. "Tell me what, my angel?"

Moving my arm free of his loose grip, I turned around, careful not to slip out on my heels. Chase looked practically regal, dressed in a fitted black tuxedo, red vest peeking from the sides. His golden blonde hair, normally messy and coated in various bits of paint, had been carefully cut and styled back, allowing his bottomless brown eyes to see everything.

I smiled, reaching up to brush the back of my hand against his cheek. "I had to tell you how amazing this is. All of it." It wasn't a lie; the entire event, from the gritty decor and artwork, to the elegant and enchanting attire. The clash of broken and perfect blended together almost effortlessly.

Cassie came to stand beside me, and out of the corner of my eyes I saw her stare at me, incredulous. "We were trying to figure out your inspiration, Cassius." Her hand found my arm, and she ran a finger down it to catch my attention. While she looked like the Cassie we knew so well, all nosy and stuck-up, the questioning look in her eyes told me she didn't understand what I was doing, why I wasn't breaking my boyfriend's heart the moment he showed up. "Care to solve the mystery for us?"

He smiled, but the action didn't quite reach his eyes. "You'll both know soon enough, but first, I need to give my toast to these fine people." He turned to me, gently lifting my chin with a finger until we locked eyes. "Don't stray too far, love."

As he blended back into the crowd, Cassie came to stand beside me, pressing herself close until we were molded as one. "What the heck was that, Essie? You said—"

"I know what I said," I fired back, scowling. "Look, I'll tell him after the event. It's fine. I don't want to crush him right now, in front of all these people. I'd look like the biggest witch this side of town."

We kept to the dark, lingering near the pool of light around the grand angel statue for our only source of light. Just when I thought we'd have to find ear plugs to cushion the deafening music from breaking our ears, the noise dimmed. Glasses clinked together, hushed voices snuffed out as everyone turned to face the grand angel statue, and the figure standing in front of it.

"Thank you, all of you, for attending on this dark and very New York evening," he started, moving over the sound of light laughter that ran through the crowd. "It has been an honor that so many of you were willing to take such precious time from your busy lives to view something as banal and overdone as art. I believe I can safely say, however, that this is art many of you have never experienced before in your lives."

I felt my attention waver, shifting uncomfortably from one heel to the next. Chase was going to go for broke, after all.

"Like many artists, I found myself inspired to create these pieces by a medium in my life. Many artists will site a quote, or perhaps a vacation spot outside of these metal buildings and concrete barriers. But I found mine in a shining star at the heart of this city." Chase steals a tiny sip of his glass before turning towards me. His eyes seemed to know exactly where I stood, and hold me hostage in my place amidst the dark. "Ladies and gentlemen, I give you the inspiration for every single piece. My own angel, and a rising star in our own social circles, Essallie Miranda Hanley."

People shift in the crowd towards my direction, and the room erupts into a soft breath of claps. Murmurs of approval wash over me and Cassie as we stand apart from the gathering near the statue. It's too much, knowing he's spotlighting me like this, putting me on a pedestal for the bizarre society of New York to gawk and needle at. My grandparents might have been proud, had they been here to watch me rise, but I wasn't them. I was more like my mother; a recluse at heart who fled to Maine to avoid the sharpened nails of high society. I immediately focus back on the tall, stony being, taking in the rigid cuts at the neck to the smooth slope of the angel's collarbones. It's elegant and frightening all at once. Again, the nagging feeling that I've seen the statue before plays in my mind, teasing my subconscious with the flickers of something... maybe a memory?

I didn't have time to think about where I've seen the angel, for Chase is suddenly approaching through the dispersing crowd. The music roared back to life with its deafening pulse, and I cringed into Cassie at the noise.

Chase's hands are steady and strong on my arm as he

reaches out for me, pulling me away from Cassie and into his embrace.

"Surprise, love. I hope I haven't embarrassed you too much," he said, lips brushing my ear before pulling back to study my face. He frowned. "What is it?"

"Nothing," I said in a rush, forcing a smile. "I'm fine, really."

He shook his head. "No, you're not." He stares past me to Cassie, narrowing his gaze. "What did you do?"

Cassie moved to defend herself, but I cut her off with a stare. "She didn't do anything, Chase, relax," I offer. "She just mentioned something about a surprise you had for me, and it's had me on edge all evening."

His eyes never look at me, staying hyper-focused on Cassie as she makes an uncomfortable shrug. "It wasn't that big of a secret."

"You never were good at keeping secrets, Cassandra," Chase said. His fingers tighten slightly on my arms, and he pulls me closer against his chest. "When will you learn?"

"That depends, Cassius," she practically growled, startling me. "When will you drop that pretentious mask of yours?"

Chase's eyes flashed, the darkness hazing in a rush of grey and silver. I had never seen anything like it before. It was then I noticed the dark bruises beneath his eyes, the sunken look of his cheeks, and the ashen color dotting the roots of his hair. What was going on?

His hands tightened enough that I let out a whimper, tugging. "Chase," I whispered nervously. "You're hurting me."

The words acted like a hot knife. Chase released me immediately, hands held out from my arm. Worry creased his eyebrows, and I felt my stomach twist at my petty need to whine.

He thrusted a hand through his hair, grimacing at himself. "What am I doing?" He murmured, head shaking. "I'm not supposed to be hurting you, I'm supposed to be..." Chase opened his eyes, warmth and kindness burning within. Tentatively, he reached for one of my hands. "I'd like to show you something, if you'll let me?"

My eyes followed to his hand, watching his fingers inch their way closer to mine. It was as if we were two magnets, drawn together by some invisible force. I felt the uncontrollable urge to cling to him with my every being, if only to push away the nagging flight urge that tingled in my legs and palms. Wrapping my hand into his, I nodded, brushing myself back against his shoulder. We nodded at Cassie, who promptly turned away and fluttered to another group of people to gossip with while her two best friends vanished.

I was surprised when Chase led us back through the entrance to his event, giving the bouncer at the front a quick nod on the way out. Chase waited patiently beside me as the elevator rolled to our floor, and once inside, he practically swallowed me in his arms, keeping my back turned to the door and face buried in his chest.

The elevator began to move, and I stumbled slightly from the jerky motion. "Where are we going?" I asked, pulling back to look up. "When Cassie told me you had a surprise, I thought she meant you painted something, or sculpted my curves from clay, or—"

He cut me off with a single kiss to the lips before chuckling in my hair. His lips brushed my forehead. "What is the point of a surprise if you know what's coming?"

The words were innocent enough, but I shivered. Instantly I thought of sinister things, of creatures with claws and fire dusted knuckles pulling me into the depths of Hell itself. It was official; I had read too many paranormal books before bed. I made the mental note to switch to a different genre next visit to the library.

Chase guided me out of the elevator once the doors opened, and I caught the faint number etched into the unpainted drywall framing the hallway. It was the seventh floor, one directly below his party. I pressed to hear the sound of thumping techno music overhead, pleased when I made out the distant noises the further we walked down the hall. He stopped at an unmarked door at the end of the hallway, gently nudging the door open and pulling me inside.

"Wait," I said, stopping just as my toes came to a halt at the frame. The unease in my stomach had gone from annoying to nauseating in seconds. Reflexively, I stepped back, heels clicking on the dusty marble floor of the hall. "I have a bad feeling about this. Chase, I don't like this at all."

Standing inside the door, he kept his hand entwined with mine. His face was half-covered in shadow as he stared at me, pouting softly.

"Essallie, would I ever do anything to hurt you?"

I automatically shook my head, lips drawn tight. He never had hurt me, not intentionally. Once or twice he had grabbed me too hard, but it was nothing I couldn't cover with long sleeves or play off as the actions of some creepy-feeling jerk on the subway. Chase wasn't violent. He couldn't hurt a fly if he tried.

Chase gently squeezed my hand. "Everything's going to be just fine, I promise."

I nodded, pushing a sigh from my lips. He was right. Cassie had been right, too. I was being ridiculous with this bad case of nerves. Maybe I was starting the downward spiral into insanity like my mother had done. The thought made me squish the remains of nerves that shook my insides, and I followed Chase into the dark without a second thought.

The door swung shut behind us, sealing us in an inky black that seemed to stretch forever in every direction. Chase's hand slipped free from my slippery grip, and I fumbled forward on my heels, cursing.

"Chase?" I whispered against the dark. I took another step forward, and my fingers ran over the rough edge of what felt like a tabletop. "Chase? Where the hell did you go? Chase!"

The nerves flared back to life with an intensity unlike any other. My body began to shake, but I couldn't tell if it was from the draft that seemed to seep up from the floorboards beneath my feet, or the chill that stilled the air as if we lived in the Arctic. Ahead, I could make out the faint sound of the city. I moved towards it, using the sound as an anchor to keep me from losing my mind in the black.

A candle flared to life to my left, and I nearly screamed, stumbling backwards. My hip slammed into something sharp, pain shooting down my leg. That was it, I was out. Chase had officially crossed the line. To be an object of art was one thing, to be lured into a dark room by your boyfriend was another? But to mess with me when I couldn't see, letting me get hurt? I was done.

"Cassius DeRapport, show your face this instant. This isn't funny," I hissed, the shout building in my voice. When he didn't answer, I finally screamed. "Chase!"

"Over here, Essie," his voice carried from across the room, closer to the noise of the city below. I inched forward, feeling in front of me as I took the tiniest of baby steps. Finally, a glimmer of moonlight sparkled into the room, and I looked up to see him standing near the only open window, half-shrouded by sheer white curtains that billowed around him.

I started to walk with more confidence, swearing like a sailor. "I hate you, Chase. Absolutely hate—" I stumbled forward as I missed a dip in the ground, and cried out. Chase had moved instantly, arms out to catch me and prop me up into his chest. The air was sucked out of my lungs from the shock, and it took me a minute to compose myself. "—I hate you so much."

He stared at me for a minute before laughing softly. "I'm sorry, angel. Did I scare you?"

"You know you did, jerk!" I punched him in the arm, satisfied when he winced. "Chase, you know I hate the dark. This isn't funny, and I don't want to be here any more. Take me back to the party."

The corners of his lips pulled down, the frown frightening on his face. His skin had pulled tighter against his face, framing his cheekbones to the point where he appeared skeletal. Dark bruises had blossomed like blush on his chin, the dark circles beneath his eyes widening until his eyes looked painted against his skin. Slivers of thin hair rimmed his collar like lingering pet hair.

I was starting to wonder if the party had taken a toll on him, from conception of his art to the very unveiling. "Chase," I said softly, reaching up to touch his face. He flinched at first, but held his place as I ran my fingertips over the paper-thin skin. "When was the last time you ate? Or slept?"

He smiled, but it didn't reach his eyes. "I'm fine, angel. Please don't worry." Lips, cracked and dry, brushed my forehead before he whispered in my ear. "As long as I have you, I'll be okay."

Oh, great. His words were going to make things that much more difficult. Gently, I freed myself from his hold, and I gave him an apologetic smile. "About that." I watched him raise and eyebrow, his dark eyes empty as I cleared my throat. "Look, Chase, I like you. I really do, but I don't think… this isn't going to work. It's not you, really, it's me." My hands reached out for his, and I pulled them close, holding them up between us. "You love me more than I love you, and it wouldn't be fair to stay in a relationship like this, holding you back. I'm sorry."

The words were easier to say than I had imagined. Still, I

knew it was going to be hard on Chase, and I stood there silently, allowing him the time to digest what I had said, hoping he wouldn't panic and try anything drastic. I didn't have my phone with me, or the tiny mace bottle I had put in my purse out of the desperate need to protect myself should I ever wander into a shady part of town. If Chase tried anything, there would be no one to hear me scream, no one to hear my cries for help. He wasn't the type to do something dangerous, just as he wasn't the type to hurt me, but the worry was still there, lingering under my words like a thin line of blood.

It felt like forever had passed when he finally moved, shifting his eyes from mine to our hands. My fingers stilled under his unwavering gaze, another chill making me shiver.

"Perhaps you're right," he said at last. His voice was soft, laced with hurt. "I had thought if I loved you hard enough, it would have been enough for the both of us. But I can see you're struggling with this. With us." He looked up at me, pulling a hand free to touch my cheek. "I'm sorry, Essallie."

Wow. That had gone over much better than I had anticipated. I swallowed before daring to speak, still swept away by how easily he was willing to let me go. "What are you sorry for, Chase? This isn't your fault. It's mine." I frowned. "But maybe we shouldn't say anything until tomorrow. This is supposed to be your night, and here I am breaking your heart like a jerk."

He pulled us away from the window, back towards the dark where the one lonely candle continued to burn. "We'll be fine, Essallie. Let them think what they want, none of them really matter. They're just…" he laughed softly. "Mortals."

The words were so bizarre, I was laughing before I could hold it back. "And what, we're not? We still live in their world, where brand names and rubbing elbows with politicians puts you at the top. We're all mortal, we're just stuck in this vain little spot."

Chase had come to a stop, turning around to catch me by the shoulders. "Essallie, do you believe there is more to this world, this life, than everything you see?"

My eyebrows bunched together, and I frowned. "Of course I do. I told you that when we first started to date." I hesitated before daring to ask, "Why?"

"Bond with me."

I went from confused to befuddled. "I'm sorry, what?"

"Bond with me," he repeated, hands still on my shoulders. "Spiritually speaking. A soul connected to another can reach out further than if it tried on its own. Imagine what you could feel, what we could feel, if we bonded our souls, connected together."

I could feel the disappointment drip down my throat, souring my stomach. Apparently I had given him too much credit for handling the break-up so well. "Chase…"

"Essallie, please." He pleaded, hand moving down to cup mine. He kissed my fingertips, his warm breath oddly calming. "I'll never ask another favor from you, not ever. Not as long as we live."

Weighing the options, I pursed my lips. If I did this, and we created some kind of bizarre, celestial bond, I wasn't sure I would be okay with that. And no doubt it wouldn't be reversible. If I didn't, Chase might grow upset and unpredictable. I wanted to kick myself for not taking my phone when we left earlier. Why was I so stupid?

"Okay," I sighed. Chase's eyes lit up like a freshly-strung Christmas tree. "But, after this, we go back to the party. No questions, no more teasing, nothing. Are we clear?"

He nodded. After that, he moved fast, shuffling me a bit further into the room where the single candle lingered, its yellow flame flickering from the movement. The lighter he pulled from his pocket was small, the cheap kind from a gas station, but it did the job. Within minutes, he had lit up the room in a dizzying display of pillar candles, casting the room in a dim, buttery glow.

Chase grabbed a small bag beside one set of candles, and began to sprinkle salt around me in a wide circle. It was then I noticed the markings already etched into the floor, written in a reddish paint. Symbols of all sorts were filled in, the outline of a star evenly set in the circle.

The nerves returned once more, and I shifted in my shoes, uncomfortable. "You do know what you're doing, right?"

"Of course," he said, sounding assured. "Why wouldn't I?"

"I've never seen anything like this. What if we accidentally open up a portal to Hell, or summon a demon, or curse me with boils for life?"

Chase laughed. "Relax. I read about this in a book I picked up from a little Wiccan shop outside the city. You won't come out with boils on your face." He came to a stop near the end of the circle, leaving a small patch free of salt. He set the bag down and stepped into the circle with me. Gently he took one of my hands, and I watched as he pressed a kiss to the palm. "You're going to be just fine."

"We're going to be just fine," I corrected him, smiling nervously. "After all, this is happening to both of us, right?"

He nodded, rubbing my palm with his thumb in slow, lazy circles. "More or less, yes."

I started to ask what he meant when I felt the pain pulse in my palm. Immediately I yanked my hand back from his and cried out. "What the hell, Chase?" I looked at my hand, stunned to see a bubble of blood that began to run along my wrist like a ribbon. It was then I noticed the small, silver dagger in Chase's hand, the blade tip coated in blood. My blood.

My head began to spin, and I swayed in my spot. Chase backed away with remarkable speed, and by the time I found focus, the circle had been closed in completely.

"Chase," I said, hearing the weakness in my voice. "You're scaring me."

His eyes had turned to the small bowl of water in front of the circle, where he dipped the blade tip into until the water turned a light shade of pink. "Sorry, love. I should have said it might hurt a little bit." He glanced up at me as he crouched before the water dish, and in the candlelight he looked possessed. "You know what they say. The best things in life come with a little pain."

"Who the hell said that?" I challenged back, shaking. I started to move toward the edge of the circle, keeping pressure on my hand. The blood had started to run over my fingers, the sticky liquid nauseating. "This is sick, you know that? I'm not doing this, I take it back. I don't want to bond with you."

A figure stepped out from the shadow, all glitter and beauty. Her voice was charming, even when she was cruel. "I wouldn't do that if I were you."

"Cassie?" I practically cried. "Oh my gosh, Cassie, go get the hotel staff, call for the police! Chase is out of his mind over here—" I paused, repeating her words in my head. "Wait, wouldn't do what?"

Her eyes flickered to Chase, and she crossed the room to him, cupping his face lovingly. "I'm sorry it took me so long. You really hurt me, you know."

"I always hurt you," he said, practically sneering. "You get too sensitive when we linger around mortals. I like you better when you take my heat and fire it back at my heart like you used to."

"Funny. Last time I did that, you whined that you'd find another Necromancer to keep your sagging excuse for a body alive." She pinched his cheek, *tsk*ing. "How's that working out for you, darling?"

Chase pushed her aside and muttered something under

his breath, and Cassie cracked a dark grin. Her eyes turned back to me as she folded her arms across her chest. "Don't take this personally, Essallie. We've been sacrificing people for decades. It comes with the deal we made forever ago." She stepped closer to the edge of the circle, and I inched closer. "I'd chalk it up to bad luck. Normally, we'd just pluck some drunken idiot off the street or from a homeless shelter. But once Chase found out what you were—"

"Cassandra," he said warningly. "You are forbidden from telling her."

She sneered back at him. "I know, I know. Always the party-pooper." Cassie flicked her eyes back to me, smug. "Let's just say, your blood is worth all the riches in the world."

They continued to bicker back and forth, lighting candles and pulling out various small bags from different corners of the room. I didn't know what to think at this point. My ex-boyfriend and best friend had to be insane. They thought magic was real? That they had to sacrifice someone? I thought back to Cassie's words about picking up drunks from bars, and started to wonder if the men she had taken to her place after our nights out ever made it back home. They were mad, absolutely out of their minds. And I wasn't going to stick around for them to kill me in their insanity.

I spotted the dagger at the edge of the circle and moved for it, reaching out to grab the hilt. As soon as my skin hit the edge of the circle, the salt lining it erupted into a wall of fire, striking my skin. I screamed and fell back onto the ground, cradling my burnt arm against my chest. What the hell was going on?

Through the flames, I heard Cassie laugh. "Should have told her she couldn't leave."

"You gave her a fair warning," Chase said. "Besides, I wanted to see if she'd actually try. Remember that girl in the 50's who tried to leave?" He sighed, and as the flames died down to a dull burn at the base of the circle, I saw him shake his head at Cassie. "She kept insisting it was a dream, burning herself over and over. I still can smell her charred flesh."

"Don't forget the boy from the orphanage," she offered, smiling blissfully. "He was precious. Do you remember when he tried to bargain with us, offering his shoes in exchange for his life?"

"If shoes kept me alive, there'd be no fun in all this killing."

"I don't know, the blood is a nice consolation prize. All that red, pooling on the floor, in the water, coating the walls…"

"Do you two hear yourselves?" I screamed, cutting them off. "You're talking about killing like people decide on what to eat for breakfast! Magic isn't real, you don't need to do this. Chase," I turned to his darkened silhouette, seeing the spark in his eyes as I called his name. "We— we can work this out. We can get you and Cassie help, I swear—"

"Help?" He incredulously asked, then laughed. "Darling, I don't need help. You might need help, well, you would if there would be anything left of you after this, but there won't be a drop of blood to identify you by. No bones, no skin, nothing. There never is when it's finished."

"There's nothing to finish!" I cried, scrambling to my feet. "I take it back, I don't want to do this, you can't keep me here!"

Chase frowned, but Cassie laughed as she stood beside him. "Sweetie, it doesn't work like that. Once you give permission and the circle is sealed, you don't get to back out. No turning back now."

"I never would have trusted you." My words were all I had left, so I was firing them as hard as I could. "I never should have trusted either of you."

"That's why we work as a team." Cassie shrugged. She

pulled a book from the table closest to her and flipped it open, shuffling through the thick cream pages. "That's why I said not to take it personally. We've perfected this over decades of trial and error. If it makes you feel any better, I will say you were one of the harder ones to lure into Chase's charm. I wonder if it has anything to do with your abilities."

"I don't have any abilities!" I shouted, squeezing my eyes shut. "Someone is going to see the smoke from these candles. The fire department will show up, and you two will be arrested for attempted murder."

Chase rolled his eyes, but when he turned to focus back on me, one eye stuck in the corner. "At which time you'll be choking on more than your misery and fear." He reached out and pulled the thick book from Cassie's hands, brushed over a few pages, then passed it back to her before sinking to the floor in a withering heap. "Hurry Cassandra, I can feel the bones dissolving in this sack of flesh."

She nodded, locking her eyes with mine, and began to chant. The words were unfamiliar, an old tongue I had never heard in my life, but the phrase she repeated was the same. With each repeat, her voice grew, stirring the air in the room. Nausea rolled my stomach flat, bile touching the back of my lips as I crouched down toward the ground, pleading.

Please don't let me die. Not here, not like this.

Just as I was about to let out another scream, the room went still. Every sound, from the faint rush of air outside the window, to the heavy breathing of Chase, vanished. One by one, the candles began to blink out, ice crusting over the wicks and shrouding the ground in a slippery rush of frost. The air slithered over my shoulder like a slimy hand, and I immediately dropped to the ground, screaming for all I was worth.

"Always with the dramatics," Cassie said, shaking her head. "Show yourself, demon, and let's get this over with."

The slithering sensation moved over my shoulder once more, and I let out another wild scream. Above me, the air danced, shifting and twisting as if something was there, but it was only a dim cloud of smoke, steadily growing as it pulled the smoke from the salt-ringed fire.

"You call upon me once more. I presume, for more time?"

The voice was dark and light all at once, slow as syrup and sour as bile. The very noise twisted my stomach to the the point of wanting to heave, and I turned my head to the side in case I would lose the battle with my gut.

From the floor, Chase's raspy voice called out to the air. "Demon! We call not just for more time, but a trade that will make us even for all eternity." He jerked his head at me, eyes bright. "The girl for eternal life. No more sacrifices."

The voice laughed, raising gooseflesh on my arms until it stung. "What could a meager mortal give me that is worth an endless supply of flesh and soul?"

"I'm so glad you asked," Cassie said, pulling a small glass tube from the side of her dress. I could make out the tiny vial and the dark liquid inside of it. It didn't take a genius to figure out it was my blood. How much of it had they stashed away, how had they taken it from me without me knowing all this time? Cassie poured the liquid out onto the floor, only to watch it burst into a rush of blue flames that leapt up at the circle as if it had hands. I scurried back as far as I could, slamming into solid air behind me and going still as the dead.

For a moment, the room was silent. Then the voice spoke, the faintest hint of amusement coloring the tone. "Agreed. It is done."

The wind in the room shifted, twisting around me like a tornado. Beneath me, the red marks flared with a hazy glow, twisting up and locking my ankles and wrists in binds. I screamed, crying out for Cassie, for Chase, for anyone to hear me. I knew it was no use, it was obvious I was going to die.

The smoke poured like a waterfall against the ground, pooling at my feet. It turned upward in a single move, shaping to a human silhouette, color bleeding into the figure as it stepped closer, closing in on me. I struggled against the binds, hyperventilating. I didn't know what I was up against, but I knew I had to try and fight. My life was going to depend on it. At least, what little life I would have left. All I knew was that I refused to go down without a bloody battle.

As the smoke cleared and the figure approached, I was almost impressed with the figure standing before me. He was handsome, the kind of look that gave off an effortless air of darkness and mystery. Deep, dark brown eyes stared into mine, matching his short raven-black hair that appeared damp from a dive in the water.

He crouched down in front of me, forcing us to lock eyes. I felt calm at once, as if someone had blotted out the need to scream and fight for every breath. He smiled, revealing rows of needle-sharp teeth and a forked tongue, and still I didn't feel the need to struggle. I was… oddly okay with dying.

"There, much better," the demon said, trying to soothe. "This will all be over before you will ever be aware of it." Long, twisted coils of smoke acted like his fingers, reaching out for my face, lingering just before touching my cheek. I wanted to close my eyes, but his gaze hold me steady, slowly drowning me in his false sense of security. The smoke reached out, and touched my face.

All at once, a blinding blue light flared within the circle, flinging me back. I felt my back crash against the ground, skin grinding over salt and fire. The air was punched from my lungs, only to be inhaled a second later as I felt the binds around my wrists and ankles shatter in another blinding burst of blue fire and light. I scrambled to my feet, fully aware I was almost lulled to my death as if it were a lullaby, and let out a wild scream.

Across the room, the figure stood near Cassie and Chase. His neck twisted to an impossible angle to study both of them. He roared, shaking the room. "What is this trickery?"

"Oh, for crying out loud," I heard Chase snap. He moved to his feet, jerking away from Cassie's hands as she tried to help his crumbling frame. Lines cut across his thin skin like deep trenches, and I could make out the beginning of an arm socket as skin peeled off his body. In minutes, he had gone from the Chase I knew and came to admire, to something out of my worst nightmare after an evening at the movies. "Take her! I offered her to you, and you agreed. Finish the deal and consume her!"

The demon stared at him, the smoke pooling on the floor turning an angry shade of red. He turned to face me, growling, and moved to touch me again. The minute his hand came in contact with my skin, blue fire rose from mine like a shield, bathing my arm in protection and scorching him. He roared in agony, the sound like shattering glass and tortured screams of the innocent, exploding into a gust of smoke that swirled to the end of the circle to take form once more. Through a patch of moonlight, I could make out sweat on the demon's temple and cheekbones as he stared me down, irate.

"Cassius," the demon called to Chase. "You have given me what I cannot touch." His eyes bled to the blackest of night as he held my petrified gaze. "There will be no deal without proper payment."

Chase's eyes widened as the demon began to dematerialize into a lazy haze of smoke. Cassie swore. "You made a deal, you are bound by your words, demon! If you leave, I'll only summon you again."

The smoke twisted within the circle, and took shape once more from the waist-up into the imitation of a human. He studied me carefully for a moment. I could hear my heart thundering in my chest, caught between shock and revelation.

This had to be all a dream, a silly dream from accidentally taking drugs. Maybe the wine had been spiked with something. But there was no way any of this was *real*. Magic wasn't real. It was the stuff of fairytales and legend, fiction books and movies on the big screen.

The top half of the demon turned back to Chase and Cassie, regarding them with the same curiosity he had just done to me. Slowly he beckoned Chase forward, and I watched as he scrambled to his thin, twig-like legs that bent like wire. He had made it three steps towards the demon when I watched the claws form on the demon's outstretched hand.

He plunged the claws into Chase's chest without a second thought, twisting his hand. The hand came free, blood smeared across the skin, Chase's still-beating heart thumping erratically in the demon's outstretched hand. Chase let out a small noise of surprise, his eyes moving from mine to Cassie's, then he slumped over to the floor, lifeless in a growing pool of his own blood.

I barely felt my ragged throat as I let out another scream. Cassie screamed, as if my own shriek had awakened her, and moved like lightning for the window. I could only watch as she jumped out the open window, a flutter of sequins and color.

Against my will, I turned back to Chase's limp body on the floor. The blood had begun to spread outward, thick dark liquid engulfing him. The demon turned to look at me, satisfaction written on his face.

"Such pity, mortals who dally with the unkind creatures of the supernatural realm," he noted, shrugging with ease. But I was still focused on the body, watching the blood move against the laws of nature as it swallowed Chase whole. Something within me screamed to move, and I stumbled to the floor past the half-formed demon, plunging my hands into the blood to latch onto Chase's form. The blood only worked faster, consuming Chase's body until nothing was left but the splatter of blood that clung to me and stained the dark floor.

I screamed. Screamed for everything I was worth. This was one dream I never wanted to have. I wanted to wake up, wanted to find myself still in bed before another day of school, find myself half-asleep at the store with Cassie as she tried on more dresses. Anything but this... because this couldn't be real.

The demon's breath was hot on my neck and ear as he leaned down to whisper. "Don't worry, little pet. You'll come to understand everything soon enough."

Seconds felt like lifetimes as I forced myself to turn toward him. "I want to wake up now. Why am I not waking up?"

"Because, Essallie, you were never dreaming to begin with." The demon smiled darkly. "This is your end and beginning all in one. Are you prepared?"

I didn't know what to say, so I turned back to the stain etched in the floor, and started to sob. Eventually, the smoke around me dispersed into thin air, vanishing like Chase's body had done before my eyes. It was then I was able to hear the sirens in the distance, the screaming growing louder and stronger in my ears. I couldn't look up to see if someone had found me in here, but it they were screaming, it had to be bad. It wasn't until the police showed up, paramedics in tow, that I learned there was only one person screaming the entire time.

It was me.

TWO
EYES WIDE OPEN

Five months later.

"Looks like you're drawing that Japanese cartoon stuff."

I looked up from my sketchbook on the desk, pencil still in mid-stride. Local Belfast hottie football runner Leonard 'Leo' Skripper was leaning over my end of the table. His head was tilted to the side, looking thoughtful at my sketch.

I took a double take around the room. Kids were slowly shuffling into the Bio classroom, some still stuffing breakfast down. And his girlfriend was missing.

"Is it supposed to be just an eye?" He looked at me.

"Umm, yeah. It's actually the only part I can really draw."

"Still," he said. "It's pretty cool. I'm sure you're not all that bad at the rest of it."

I fought back a snort. "It's a little odd to start talking to your neighbor after six weeks of stone cold silence."

"Happened in that vampire book."

40

I was impressed he even knew what a book was, much less a popular novel. "That was because he wanted her blood. You just want me to move seats."

"Actually I was trying to politely invite you to my house party I'm having tonight."

I blinked. Part of me wondered if he had actually just said that or if I had hallucinated it. Turning back to my sketch I focused on shading the inside of the eye. "Sorry. Not really the people-person type."

Out of the corner of my eye I watched him run his hand through his hair and frown. "We're having this big bonfire in my new backyard. S'mores and music. You sure?"

He was trying to be nice, and I knew inwardly I should have accepted his invite and just decided not to show. But my bitter attitude was spreading like an infectious germ. "I'll pass. Why come into the contact of alcohol and drunken handsy-horny boys when I can stay chaste and sober at home?" I turned my gaze to him and gave my best screw-off smile.

Leo opened his mouth to talk when Mr. Whitley threw open the classroom door. He carried in a large brown box which he quickly dropped onto the nearest front table.

"Alright, wake-up, shape-up, let's go. Mark stop texting and Leo if you keep that mouth open long enough a bird will make a nest in it. Or I'll make a nest for it and keep you outside in the courtyard." He shuffled behind his desk and after a quick role call went back to his box.

"As you all know," he began. "This is Bio II. And unlike most of your teachers here, I aim to actually teach you something you will take with you into the big bad world out there. And today, we learn anatomy."

I rolled my eyes. Anyone who thought a sixteen year old didn't know what humans had, anatomically speaking, was an idiot. I flipped open my sketchbook and went back to work.

Mr. Whitley continued, "Over here in my pretty little

cardboard box will be your projects for the day." He rustled inside the box and pulled something out in plastic. The girls in the front row squealed. "By dissecting a cat we can learn so much more of what rests inside of the corpse."

My pencil broke.

"When I give you your cat, it's going to come in a bag like this. You're going to open it at the top, pull out the cat, and using the tool sets in the back cabinets, you'll slice open the chest cavity to view all the major organs."

The room began to spin. Flashes of torn flesh and smeared blood blotted out the classroom, the smell of sweat and copper overpowering my nose.

"Once you get past that, I want you to open all the limbs. Look at the muscle, the bone."

My fingernails were digging into the corner of the table. The smell was growing sharper and more metallic with each second.

"And, if you have time before the end, I want you to explore the skull. Hell, if it interests you enough you can de-brain the cat and take the skull home."

I couldn't take it anymore; I bolted from the classroom. In the hallway, I pressed myself against the cool wall of lockers, swallowing repeatedly. Flashes of grinning white teeth decorated in candy-red blood forced themselves to the front of my brain. Laughter danced in my ears.

I opened my eyes. The demon stood before me, holding Chase's glistening spine in one hand. His eyes never left mine as he trailed his tongue over the ridges of each disc. I clamped a hand over my mouth and sprinted for the nearest bathroom, making it just inside the stall before I lurched over the toilet and heaved.

Only four months remained of my senior year and it looked like there wasn't a prayer in my direction. How could I focus in class when everything I saw connected to that night?

Ever since the ritual I had been seeing the demon everywhere, not a hair out of place. He never did anything to me, just smiled and made sure to leave me screaming for my sanity. It wasn't exactly easy to explain to everyone that I saw an imaginary creature holding chunks of my dead ex-boyfriend to play with like jump rope.

I placed the toilet lid down and sat atop it, knees hugging to my chest. It had been nearly six weeks since my last vision-attack. Part of me had been hoping I could put it all in the past. Lead a normal life with college, boyfriends, the things a 17-year-old should be focusing on. Instead, I was spending my time avoiding anything remotely triggering and barely passing school, all while some creature stood behind me and pulled the strings.

From the bottom of the stall I watched three pairs of feet walk in, chatter of a party, make-up and other things filling the silence, giggling as they went about their conversation. How easy it would be if the only thing I had to worry about was the zit forming on my forehead, or if I was going to dress up for spirit week.

"All of you, out," someone said from the door. A pair of feet dressed in imitation-destroyed Doc Martens walked in. "That means leave. If I need to offer a definition, just imagine what your Daddy did to Mommy when he found out she was a gold-digger."

Silence. One of the original three muttered something under her breath before half-shoving through the door. The Doc Martens stopped in front of my stall and knocked twice, paused, then knocked twice more.

"Occupied," I said.

"I know it's occupied you twit, they sent me to find you. Open the door," she snapped. One of her feet began to tap impatiently.

"What if I'm naked?"

"Trust me honey, it's nothing I haven't seen. Artist, remember? I doodle nudes for the hell of it."

I had to laugh at that. Only Abigail could make a joke about drawing a penis for a living and not snort. The latch came unhinged and the door swung open.

Abigail may have only stood just shy of five feet, but she was known for being a talker-backer, a take-no-shit girl with wit to match tongue. Blemish-free ivory skin and dye-job crimson red hair only made her freakishly large almond-colored eyes stand out more. Today she sported one of her favorite outfit combinations; a floor-length peasant skirt and an oversized chunky grey sweater. An armful of bangles jingled against another as she placed her hands on her hips.

"You look like hell, Essie," she said, eyeing me up and down. She extended a hand and helped me to my feet to brush off my clothes. "What was it this time?"

"Whitley and his damn dissections," I sighed. "I was doing so well, too. So much for ditching the weird girl tag." One of the mirrors caught my eye as we walked out. The girl that stared back looked hollow. Parchment white skin blending with a pixie crop of honey blonde hair and brown eyes that looked like bottomless pits. I looked nothing like the smiling girl that used to stare back at me before everything went to hell; no make-up to frame the eyes, no blush to bring life to my cheeks. It was only fair I looked as I felt.

Abigail steered me away from the mirrors and out of the bathroom. Class bells chimed overhead, signaling the end of fourth period. "Good, lunch. You need the break."

I stared at her. "Do I look that bad?"

She didn't miss a beat. "Absolutely. Cross combo of starving Ethiopian and abandoned puppy."

"Please, don't sugar coat it for my benefit," I said with a glare. We turned right and passed through the main hall to cross into the Cafeteria. Abigail's friends were already seated, munching over lunch and sketchbooks and textbooks.

"I'm heading up for food. You want something?" she asked. I shook my head. No point in trying to risk eating after losing breakfast to the toilet bowl.

I took my seat at the table silently, offering a small smile to anyone who looked up at me. Most of Abigail's friends kept to themselves, preferring to act like I was more of a temporary cinch in their lives than a future graduating peer. Still, it was a small step up from rejected outcast like the rest of the district had offered me.

Abigail set her tray down and took the seat alongside me. "I miss anything good in History, Thomas?"

The slender boy across the table looked up and shook his head, his chestnut brown hair moving in waves. "Hart bumped back the project to next Tuesday." His eyes darted to my face for a moment before returning to her. "Guess we've got time for the party after all."

"You mean Leo's party?" I asked, recalling the conversation moments before Whitley and his evil box came in.

Hesitation stained Thomas' green eyes. "Yeah, that's the one," he finally said. "Did he tell you?"

I nodded, recalling Leo's pearly whites and perfectly pressed varsity jacket. "In Biology. Just before I had the pleasure of seeing what a hairless dead cat looks like."

He snorted, the corners of his mouth twitching up. "Whitley was never known to be a man of sensitivity."

Abigail swallowed a bite of her french toast before raising an eyebrow at me. "Excuse me, but when did Leonard ask you to this party? Did his girlfriend say anything?"

"Pay attention. I said this morning. And his girlfriend was too busy looking like she wanted to rip my face off and use it to wipe her new designer shoes to say anything," I shrugged. I took Abigail's water bottle and took a sip. "No biggie."

"No biggie, please. You think he just asks everyone to his parties?" She rolled her eyes and took back the water bottle to take a swig. "Thomas only heard through the ever-infamous social grapevine. You'd best go. Maybe if they saw you outside of school you could lose your weird girl association."

I shook my head. "I'm a reformed party-goer. Besides, I have a feeling if I showed up I'd end a lot like *Carrie* did."

Abigail shrugged her shoulders and finished her last bite of lunch. "Suit yourself." She stood up and took her tray, the others all following suit.

The rest of the day went by without a hitch. If you count ducking every question and insult thrown my way. As I stepped on the bus and watched us leave, I caught sight of Leo kissing his girlfriend, my stomach clenching. There was no way I would belong at his party, or anyone's party for that matter. The entire school was so grossly perfect in their own way that it sickened me to the core. Going would only exaggerate the awkwardness and further prove how little I fit into their small-town life.

If only I'd said that about the last party I'd been to.

THREE

BY BLOOD WE BIND

I was pretty sure the disaster in front of me was going to make it on one of Jayson's Top Ten Worst Moments to Trust Me With Cooking. Smoke filled the kitchen, swirls of white covering the navy walls and stainless steel counter tops. I looked in distaste at the pile of half-burnt, half-raw eggs hissing in the frying pan.

Footsteps sounded in the hallway. Jayson poked his head around the corner, coughing vigorously. "What in God's green Earth are you doing, Essie?"

I turned around and stared into the clouded space, doing my best not to cough. "Making dinner?"

He sighed and stepped into the kitchen, taking the wash towel off my shoulder. With the window over the sink cracked open he started to fan the smoke outside. "Well, one thing's for sure. You definitely have Mom's inability to cook down pat."

"Funny," I sneered and placed the burnt pan into the sink. The cold water only added more smoke to the air but I ignored it. "Better to not know how to cook than to sound like her." I watched him blush as his jaw hardened.

"Excuse me, little sis, but don't you remember how the saying goes?"

"Sticks and stones can break my bones-"

His head shook. "Give a man a meal, he'll be fed for a day. Teach him to cook and he'll be fed for life." He gave me his best mocking face amidst the haze. "You're already looking a little peaky there."

I sighed and shut off the water, twisting the knob until it felt like it'd never budge again. "Truce and order pizza?"

"Thought you'd never ask."

I could feel the grin slipping on my lips before I even realized it. "I'll call." The number was on the fridge, scribbled on a piece of yellow construction paper with blue sharpie.

It had been easier than I thought it would be to get along with my half-brother than I had expected. Abigail had given me tips the first month of school, little pieces of information on him I had used like gold nuggets. Surprisingly, it hadn't been hard to stick to his no-party lifestyle and eat bowls of cereal in front of the fish tank in the middle of the night out of boredom. He had made sure returning to the House of Horrors as we called it wasn't nearly as traumatizing as it had been the last time we lived in it. Back when Mom wandered the hallways at night swearing her children were possessed by the devil.

Jayson came over to the fridge, pan in his hand. "Really, Essie? You burnt eggs? Who burns eggs?"

I shrugged but laughed at his expression. "Your face tells me I'm the first."

"You may very well be in the history of humanity." He put the pan back in the sink and turned around to lean against the counter. "Pizza on the way?"

"Yep. Twenty minutes until we're stuffing our faces with

slices of cheesy saucy bread littered in mushroom and pineapple chunks." Sitting down at the small table in the corner of the kitchen my eyes landed back on the History assignment I abandoned originally to a growling stomach. I really wasn't looking forward to answering about the Holocaust and WWII when I had already covered it in 9th grade in NYC.

Jayson peered over the table at my paper load. "You'll honestly never need to know any of the stuff they teach you in that class. When are you really going to need to know about people looking like underweight animals?"

"Beats the hell out of me," I shrugged and chewed on the end of my pencil eraser. "We also didn't need to fill our heads with the Salem Witch Trials. Like the devil really sat in those girl's souls."

"But you have to admit the Crucible was a good movie," Jayson said. The doorbell went off and he went to fetch the pizza while I recalled Winona Rider's face, crying that everyone was a witch and trafficked with the devil.

Jayson came back into the kitchen pizza box in hand, an amused expression on his face. "That Walker kid sure had ants in his pants. Something about a party down the way that he can go to if no one else calls in the next few hours." He shook his head. "Kids, all about the local kegger."

I bit the inside of my cheek and kept my eyes to my homework. "I think I know what party he's going to."

"Oh?" Jayson opened the pizza box and grabbed the largest slice, biting into it like a steak. "Who's hosting?"

"The Skripper kid, Leo," I said, the morning replaying in my head. "Didn't mention any kegs, though."

"You know better," he got out between bites. "Any High School party is going to have some kind of alcohol, be it from the parent's cabinet or paying off the local brewer for a few sets. Isn't that what they did in New York?"

ILLUMINE

I practically snorted. "Not even close." You didn't have to bribe anyone to get your hands on a bottle of whiskey in the city. All you had to do was find a homeless guy looking for a couple extra bucks and maybe a bottle or two of whatever you were having. Unless you had an older friend in college who'd take off with half the supply from every party they hit coming to yours. That was the easiest way to get a mix of everything.

I looked up from my homework to see Jayson thoughtfully chewing. Better to strike while the iron was still hot. "What if I had wanted to go?"

"Mmf fanfwer mmmf shhtill me fuf," he sputtered. I shook my head until he swallowed and repeated. "The answer would still be no."

Of course not. It didn't matter if I was smart, neurotic, or even mentally insane, he wouldn't budge.

"It's for your own good, really," he said in a low tone. Another slice found its way for his mouth.

"Really?" I could feel the hairs on the back of my neck rise, the words jumping off my tongue, ready to condemn me on the spot. "Because socializing with my peers isn't for my good, not at all. Where'd you read that, Jayson? The back of a cereal box?"

"Actually your grandparents," he snapped, bits of mushroom sputtering from his lips. He forced another mouthful down before he spoke. "Don't look so surprised. They told me all about having to get you from a party a week after the in-"

I felt the color drain from my face. Shaking I stood up, pushing my papers into a pile. Slick palms made it impossible. "Great. Who the hell else knows, who? The principal, the shrink, the whole damn student body?" No wonder I was avoided like the plague, everyone was too busy swapping horror stories of my mental breakdown behind my back.

"That's not what I meant, Essallie," he said. He placed a

hand on top of mine as I jerked back. "They just don't want to see your hurt. You're in a difficult place, we get that. But I don't want to have to come get you in the middle of the night because of some unforeseen trigger."

"You're impossible," I snarled and shoved the chair into the table. "Did you ever think all of this, this place, these people, the ever-elusive House of Horrors, all of it is one giant trigger waiting to happen?" I threw my hands in the air. "Maybe they should have just locked me up. At least I wouldn't have to look at all of this anymore."

"Essallie," Jayson rose from his chair, sorrow in his eyes. "Please."

"No Jayson. You had your chance, just like Mom. We all had our chance to be normal." I headed for the door, stopping only to look over my shoulder. Jayson was still standing there, watching, waiting maybe for me to run back into his arms and become the sister he wanted, become the siblings we should have been all those years ago. "Guess I'm more than Mom than you knew, right down to the asylum-worthy behavior."

Bedroom door shut and locked, I stared ahead at the far wall from the door. The same peach colored walls with cream molding trim and lace curtains stared back at me like they had all those years ago. If I closed my eyes I could almost make out the sane little girl I once was, hiding from a mother that had become drastically unstable.

Lights came through the window over my desk, the faint sound of an engine turning on hitting my ears. I walked across the room and pulled back the curtains watching Jayson pull out of the driveway and leave. I bit my lip and reached for my cell phone, his number third on speed dial. But what would I say to him? I'm sorry I'm mentally unstable? Sorry you got stuck with me because someone tried using me as bait for an evil I can't point out without being locked away?

I hit the first button. It picked up on the second ring.

"Essie? You in trouble?" The voice asked.

"Want to go to a party tonight?" I said. Turning to the mirror I caught my reflection. A sparkle of mischief danced in my eyes, my lips curving into a Cheshire smile.

The other line was quiet for a moment, but when the voice answered there was a pleased tone about it. "About time you step up to the plate," Abigail commented. "Be ready in five."

FOUR
A PACT WITH THE DEVIL

Across the small town of Belfast, Maine sat the only development of 'luxury' homes. House upon house of perfectly decorated brick, stone, and wood gave the place an eerie Stepford-wives feel. Leo's parents were two of the town's most known socialites. One a high-profile TV face and the other a former NFL player, they claimed the only way they could continue to live in Belfast was to build a gated home in a complex surrounded by others like themselves. Word had it his parents paid for the whole complex, houses and all, just for the township to approve it. The women I sat behind at church put it a little more bluntly: they bribed the town with enough money to make Bill Gates blush.

By the time Abigail and I got there, the party was in full swing. Kids sat half-past-drunk on the lawn, empty party cups strewn everywhere. Strobe lights flashed from the windows of the massive mansion, music blaring loud enough to spill out across the lawn to the street. A quick peek inside showed kids altering between body shots off the cheerleaders or chugging contests. All they needed was a back room with some alcohol

IV bags ready to go and no one would be left sober.

We stepped inside the house, crossing over a couple in the midst of a sloppy make-out session. Beside me Abigail looked almost fearful. "You sure you want to be here? Cops could show up any minute," she half-screamed over the music.

I shook my head. "Cops don't crash a Skripper party, no way, no how." A puddle at the end of the flickering hall looked like water, or maybe vomit. "Come on, maybe there's more in the back."

We took turns watching our step between the broken objects, sloppy drunks, and weird pyramids of party cups throughout the house. Three different living rooms, two accidental walk-ins to bedrooms, and one broken lamp later, we were safely behind the kitchen doors. Oddly enough the kitchen looked like the only untouched room in the whole house. The music had dimmed to a low background noise.

Abigail ran her fingers along the white marble countertops as she walked to the fridge and pulled out a bottle of water. Popping the top off she asked, "Was that really Ashley Jacobs doing-"

I shuddered and sank into one of the wicker bar stools at the island counter. "Yes, yes it was."

We busted out laughing. She paused between sips of water to admire the bottle in her hands. "Good to know her gag reflex is still functioning, very well too I may add." Her laugh turned into a snicker. "Wait until Brady-boy finds out."

I blinked and stared. "You mean that wasn't her boyfriend?"

She let out a cackle and shook her head. "Most definitely not! Brad has a," she paused. The outside sliding door had opened, Leo slipping inside. His green eyes widened in surprise as he took in the sight of the Abigail, only to stop and stare at me.

"Ah, the host finally shows!" Abby raised her water bottle.

"Cheers. You managed to get every student in Belfast High sloshed."

He chuckled, sparing her a shake of the head. But his eyes came back to rest on me. "Not my doing. Some other guys from the team brought the booze. Ryan and his buddies bled their parents' cabinets dry." He passed Abby and took a can of soda from the fridge. "The remaining of us that are sober are at the bonfire out back. You two going to join?"

Abigail and I exchanged glances. I had already came and proved my point to Jayson that I wasn't nuts and going to split in half on the turn of a dime. And so far the hallucinations had been keeping to themselves which was twice as nice. No harm in a little fun.

"I came this far, might as well go all the way," I grinned and winked at the two of them, hopped off the stool and gave Leo a stare. "Lead the way."

He nodded and opened the door but not before I caught the twitch of a smile on his lips. We followed him out into the inky night, small lanterns hanging on iron rods illuminating an endless backdrop of meticulously manicured backyards. Cobblestone paths spiraled and twisted every which way, leading to anything from a personal sauna to an emergency bomb shelter compound, Leo told us. I believed it.

Just over the hill a yellow-glow bled over the horizon line. Leo led us closer until we reached the peak of the hill. Just below the slope a giant bonfire, chunks of wood as the size of ancient tree trunks piled into the shape of a frame for an Indian tee-pee stood ablaze. Streaks of red, orange, yellow and blue wrapped around the wood like a vice, encasing it in its eternally burning grasp.

Leo continued down the slope without us, reaching his girlfriend and giving her a small kiss on the cheek. Her eyes turned to me and narrowed to slits almost instantly.

"What is your beef exactly with Ursula?" Abigail asked.

We joined the others in front of the fire, most preferring to avert their eyes than greet us.

I shrugged. "I'm the social discrepancy intruding her perfect little world." When Abigail stared back at me, I rolled my eyes. "I'm the bug in her bedroom hanging above her head. Duh."

As if she had sonic hearing, Ursula cleared her throat. "*So* surprised to see you here, Hanley. I thought the picture of a dead cat on the front door would have left you screaming."

Snickers rebounded around the bonfire. My cheeks flushed and I looked to Leo, who pointedly looked away. He looked just as embarrassed as me.

Over the thrumming roar of the flames, I sharpened my tongue. "Funny, Ursula. Get that off the box your tacky fashion-sense came from? Or did your over-paid hairstylist tell you to say that?" I gave a nonchalant shrug and stage whispered. "I'd consider hiring a new one. She makes you look 30 with that crop cut."

Ursula pursed her lips, narrowing her eyes even further. "Why did you run, Hanley? Afraid the teacher was going to use you for dissection next?"

"I'll give you a dissection," Abigail muttered, stepping forward. I grasped one of her wrists and shook my head. It just wasn't worth it. One look around the bonfire told me that everyone else was with Ursula on this. My thoughts from before were true, I didn't belong here. I was invading their space, their lives.

All I wanted was for the kids to quit thinking I was a freak. To include me in their circles, maybe not a friend, but not an outcast. Heat spread through my skin, building in my fingertips and cheeks. Just once, I wanted to fit in somewhere, wherever it would be.

I pulled my hands back and shouted. My fingertips were tender and red, almost blistering. I must have had my hands too close to the fire. I looked around, waiting to hear the bursts of laughter for being the only one to scald myself on the fire, but it seemed no one had even noticed.

"Hey, Essallie, did you need my notes for Biology?" someone called out from across the fire. A couple people stepped aside as one of the girls, Emily Sanders I remembered, came over with a shy smile on her face.

"Uhhh, you sure?" I looked at Abigail, who shrugged but gave me the same raised eyebrow look. Emily was one of Ursula's 'clones', as we called them privately. They matched in almost everything, from clothing choices to taste in boys. I took a quick glance over towards Ursula just in time to watch her face turn to a violent hissing mask of rage.

"Yeah, I'm sure. Gabby and I both did it. You know, one does the first half while the other does make-up, then we switch," she giggled, her smile growing more with each word she spoke. "And," her voice dropped low, "if you need anyone to talk to about, you know, all that weird stuff that happened in New York, I know a few of the student councilors."

Weird stuff. Good to know the rumors were still flying around like hawks for the kill. "Weird stuff?"

"Yeah," someone else piped up. I recognized him from Math, Dalton was his name. He seemed to hesitate for a second. "But it's all just rumor, right? You didn't really get bit by a vampire and take off out the window with wings from your back, right?"

A redhead who I didn't know made a noise. "I heard you were bathed in dead animal blood. That's why you ran from the Bio classroom, or so Jessica said."

The blonde alongside the redhead, Jessica I presumed, shook her head. "No you idiot, I said she ran because the dissection reflected what was going to happen to her once the ritual began." Her chest swelled up as she tried to look important. "A god can only wait so long for a sacrifice."

I listened to all of it, watching as each one spelled out a different rumor. One had me as a hybrid human, another as an alien, some even thought I was probed by aliens. Any mythical creature, both the known and unknown, were called into the air. It was all I could do not to laugh myself to death. Abigail on the other hand, was in hysterics.

"What about angels?" one voice called out. A couple heads turned as I strained to see who it was that had asked. Across the bonfire, dressed like everyone else, stood a familiar face. Too familiar. I already knew without having to stand beside him that his skin was a dark olive color, perfectly unblemished. His eyes could be whatever color his heart desired, but grey and black were the only two I'd ever imagined in my hallucinations.

I had gone too far.

"Excuse me, who are y-" Ursula started to snip.

"I asked the girl. Essallie, is it?" The demon gave me the best harmless smile his vicious features could manage. A wolf in sheep's clothing.

All eyes turned from the demon to me. He wasn't just a hallucination this time, I realized. Everyone else could see him, too. In one decision I had inadvertently placed every person in my contact directly into his hands. Hands with claws like steel, ready to rip flesh off like tissue paper off a gift on Christmas morning.

My mouth was dry as I spoke. "Yes, Essallie. Who are you, again?"

"Who I am is not important."

I shook my head. If he was willing to interrupt my life to slaughter those around me, I'd stall him as long as I could in my only gutsy move. "Oh no, boy, it is. Tell me your name and then we'll begin the game."

Abigail beside me whispered 'Game?' into my ear, but I ignored her. My eyes were locked onto the demon, waiting for the slightest hint of movement. He let out a small, infuriated sigh and ran his fingers through the short black hair on his head, but his smile never faltered. If anything, it only grew larger across his cheeks. "I love games. What game will we be playing, Essallie?" He purred, letting his s's roll.

"War," I said, picking the first game that came to mind. "For the last time, you are who?"

His eyes smoldered, seeming to burn hotter than the fire between us. "Kayden."

All around us I felt each pair of eyes bouncing back and forth, a never-ending tennis match of words and hidden exchanges. "Alright, Kayden. The answer is no, no one has suggested angels. Pretty sure that's the opposite of sacrifices and buckets of blood. Especially when the guy who tried to kill me used a demonology book, not the Bible."

"Actually," Jessica snuck back into the conversation, "there's tons of sacrifice and blood in the Bible. It's just not actively capitalized on."

The demon, Kayden, cut her off. "Save the Bible Study chat for Sunday School, little girl."

"Excuse me," Ursula growled, the shiver of fear from Jessica fueling my own inner fire. "We don't tolerate playground bullies around here. Or party crashers for that matter. Leo's buddies will escort you out."

Two of the football players from our school stepped close to him. Kayden looked from one to the other, a sly smile creeping on his lips. As one of the players grasped Kayden's upper arm, Kayden ducked underneath and between the guy's legs, using his other hand to pull him down face first into the mud.

In another move, he stood in front of Ursula, pitch black eyes piercing into hers. "Essallie," he called, never looking to me. "I'd let your little friend here in on the secret you learned the first time we met."

I could still grasp onto the beads of courage bubbling inside my chest, but barely. My skin started to turn cold, the hairs standing up on the back of my neck. Somewhere inside I knew the answer to my question, but I asked regardless. "What secret?"

When he turned to face me for all of one second, it took all of me not to scream. His face had transformed into a mask of horror, scales lining his previously unblemished skin like craters. Little horns of pure onyx encircled his face as extra nostrils covered his nose. But I was solely focused on the needle-thin razor teeth, yellowed from time, and the set of pure black eyes that encompassed nearly half of his face, the insides bubbling crimson vats.

Only one eye blinked, specks of blood flicking off his short eyelashes. "That I pick my teeth with weaklings like all of you."

As fast as the mask had shown itself, he returned to perfectly normal. No one else seemed as terrified as I was, so I knew he only let me see the gruesome face. Slowly he stepped back, his eyes trailing over every person huddles around the bonfire. The flames had suddenly began to die, glimmers of the wintry frost of Maine coating the corners of each log.

He was threatening to kill every one of them, just like he had Chase.

All because I had associated with them. Because he couldn't touch me for reasons unknown.

Rage began to build inside my chest. How dare he try to take away the only remaining pieces of a normal life I had left? And for what, so he could eat me? Adrenaline pumped through my veins, and it was all I could do to not see red. The burn of untamed energy spread through my body once again, building in my fingertips like pressure points ready to burst. No more mercy, no more running. I was done.

"Go ahead and try," I hissed and stepped closer to him.

Behind me I felt the flames from the bonfire burst skyward with a gust, blowing concentrated heat over my shoulders.

Kayden's smirk slipped, an emotionless mask falling in place. He opened his mouth to speak when a scream sounded behind me.

I turned. Jessica was laid out on the ground, eyes rolled up in the back of her head. Her body quivered and shook involuntary, limbs splaying out every which way. Abigail, Ursula, Leo, and the others immediately moved to her, holding her down and keeping her head in place. "Someone call an ambulance!"

Ursula had her phone cradled against her cheek, giving the operator Leo's address. First responders would be on their way in minutes, along with the local Belfast police chief, Jessica's father.

I turned back around. Kayden was gone. But where he stood the grass was missing, only scorched ground remained.

FIVE
THORN IN YOUR SIDE

The next morning seemed darker, drearier. Like curtains blocking the sun from a room, Belfast's skies acted like a veil, obscuring everything into a hollow of an abyss. Its effect was visible all around; it seemed to seep into everyone, myself included.

I stood outside Abigail's locker just before lunch. She continued to rifle through the same stack of papers crammed awkwardly into the corners of her locker, grumbling under her breath with each shove of stuff. Even she was unnaturally short-tempered today. I couldn't help but feel Kayden had something to do with the gloomy attitude lingering over the school.

No. I was not about to go there. Excusing a poor weather day on a supernatural creature, if they even really existed, was not something I was going to start doing. There was always a real reason for the way things happened, like physics and psychology. Kayden was probably just some figment of my imagination everyone else was engaging with last night out of pity. Or maybe last night never happened at all.

"So how bad did you get the third degree last night?" I asked Abigail, trying and keep my mind off creeping thought of Kayden. That, and the thought that maybe I was going completely bat-shit insane.

"What? Oh, please." Abigail stuck her head out of her locker, having cussed in a low breath. Her hand waived dismissively at my face. "Like my Mom cares if I come home. She's too busy trying to hook a man to *give me the father I deserve.*"

"That's disturbing."

"That's my Mom's way of life. Sleep, bait, screw, then plead for marriage." She shook her head disappointingly. "What about you? I'm sure Jayson didn't go easy."

I almost groaned. *Didn't go easy* barely captured his reaction. After having the wonderful pleasure of him being one of the first responders to show, things weren't really smooth between us, but more like a cluster of grunts. The words 'grounded' and 'banned' had been heavily mixed in with all kinds of other lovely phrases.

"Let's just say this; if I go missing in the next few weeks, make sure Jayson is investigated. And the backyard dug up," I added morbidly. Inside her locker, Abigail snorted.

"He's just protecting you the best way he knows how. You know how it is in the movies? The older brother's always afraid his cute little sis is going to choke on the marshmallow, or drown in her closet of clothes," she cracked in between giggles.

I swatted the back of her head, hearing her swear. Sadly, Jayson was exactly the person to worry I would choke on a marshmallow, or worse, break a bone falling on a wad of pillows. "He's more afraid I'm going to choke on air, or something stupid like that. I think he even glued my window pane shut the other night just in case." Not that I wasn't guilty of tripping into things, everyone was. But at least I could say I had never fallen out of a window, open or closed.

Swearing for a different reason, Abigail slammed her locker shut, kicking it for good measure. "Come on, we're going to be late for lunch. And while we're on the subject, think of a good excuse as to why I can't find my Bio paper so Whitley doesn't fail me."

"Tell him you had to work the corner last night to get over your Daddy issues," I suggested with barely controlled laughter. Abigail glared. "Sorry, I got nothing. I'm still replaying last night in my head."

"What are you, a DVD player?" She grinned, shaking her head as we walked into the Cafeteria and took our usual seats. Like always, we were the last two, and from the looks of it, no one was in the mood to offer any form of communication. At least, not while I, the resident danger-magnet, was around.

Abigail dropped her brown bag lunch on the table. Today was a sandwich of tuna on wheat, a homemade blueberry muffin, and a travel mug of lukewarm cocoa. She broke the silence before taking a bite of the muffin. "Any news on Jessica?"

I sat back with a notebook on my lap, choosing to play wallflower. Thomas spoke first. "She's still in Portland, last I heard. They're running CT scans, looking for why she had the seizure."

"Think it had anything to do with that Kayden kid who was creeping on Essallie?" One of the girls I met last night, Emily, chimed in as she sat alongside Thomas. She appeared drastically different today, sporting a tan turtleneck and wine colored floor length skirt. It was a far cry from her normal attempt to copy Ursula with denim miniskirts and curve-hugging spaghetti strap tank tops.

I stopped in mid-Algebra equation and looked up, my palms suddenly sweating. "What about Kayden?"

"Why don't you tell us, Essallie?" Thomas challenged, narrowing his eyes. "You were the only one there who knew him."

"There's no need for the hostility, Thomas," Abigail chided.

I put my hand out in front of Abigail, shaking my head. "I got this, Abby, thanks. Thomas, what do you think? That I knew he was going to crash the party? I know him just about as much as all of you. We've only met once."

"Funny," he said. "You two flickered like two halves of a flame coming together again."

I pursed my lips. "Your attitude is really uncalled for. You're making me out to look like I intended for him to fight with me and cause Jessica's seizure."

"It's just a little surprising how well he knew you, considering you've claimed to only have met once." He leaned forward, implications screaming from his eyes. "Unless that one time encounter was a less conversation, a little more action?"

"Thomas!" Abigail shouted, narrowing her eyes in anger. "What the hell has gotten into you?"

"What's gotten into me? How about what's gotten into you?" Thomas turned his budding fury to Abigail, the flames in his eyes unmistakable. "Here you are, not even doing your *job* and letting her associate with that- that-"

"That what?" Abigail hissed. "Go ahead, say it. Ruin everything and say it."

His lips curled, a sneer so fierce on them, it would have curdled dairy. "All I will say is this. You're walking a fine line, Abigail, and she'll figure it all out sooner rather than later."

I stood from my seat and placed my hands on the lunch table, leaning far enough to touch noses with Thomas. The way he was threatening Abigail wasn't just weird, it was past my point of comfort. "Leave her out of this, Thomas. You want to ask Kayden why he seems to be so smitten with me, be my guest. Good luck finding him, though."

"He doesn't have to look far."

Thomas and I both turned to Emily. She shifted in her seat uncomfortably, pointing toward the double doors of the Cafeteria. The confidence she had displayed earlier had reduced to a dull mumble. "He's right there."

"What?" I turned around, part of me hoping Emily was bluffing, the other part wishing for a pickaxe. Dressed in jeans and a half-undone button up, he blended right in with every other guy on the ads in New York. Compared to the student body of Belfast he stood out like a sore thumb, his dark skin cleaner than the streaked orange look most of the wannabe tanners sported, but still foreign to the pale faces typically seen in the community. In other words, he was a giant gossip magnet.

And he was heading straight for me. Great.

"Abigail, give me something to hit him with," I growled under my breath, grasping for anything on the chair beside her. I locked my fingers around something heavy and thick-paged. As soon as he rounded the corner to our table, I threw it.

His hand came up, catching the textbook with an inhuman easy grasp of the fingers, and continued to walk over. He *tsk-tsk'd* once he stopped in front of our table, leaving just enough space between us that I couldn't reach for him.

"Nice to see you again, Essallie," he spoke smooth, like melting butter on a hot pan, moving with the same silky attitude as he deposited Abigail's book on her lap. "Shame, you having to resort to primal violence in a desperate attempt to cover your emotions."

Thomas shot me a glare, mouthing the words, "I knew it."

I started to see red.

Against her better judgment, Abigail snickered. Still, she

played cool, keeping the role of the levelheaded one between my fiery temper and his icy sheen. "What brings you to the small cavernous hole of Belfast?"

His head tilted to the side, a playful smile stretching his lips. "Let's just say it wasn't by choice."

Bells rang overhead, end of lunch. I wasted no time scooping up my things and making like mad animal to my next class.

But as soon as I stepped into the English Literature classroom, I knew something was off. Everyone was either standing or leaning against the walls with their messenger bags on the floor. Whispered conversations floated between the small clusters of people spread throughout the room.

I spotted Emily in the back, leaning on the windowsill with Ursula alongside her. Both sported bored expressions. "What's going on?"

Emily shrugged, the paranoia of Kayden's arrival seemingly worn off. "No teacher. Looks like a study hall day." She glanced over to the kids skipping out of the room. "Or an excuse to cut, it seems."

Go figure. The one day I actually need a little distraction in the form of Shakespeare and Poe, and I can't have it. I glanced up at the clock on the wall. Only two more hours left of school, might as well head home to avoid every chance possible of seeing Kayden.

Slipping out with a few others, I made sure to hit my locker for all my extra books and homework before I left through the Cafeteria. The small patch of outdoor picnic tables led me straight to the parking lot for students, leaving for a slim chance to run into anyone.

"Essie."

Or so I thought.

"Essie."

And now he has a nickname for me. My hunter, my

demon, gave me *a goddamn nickname.* I'd throttle him into the next millennium.

I didn't bother to look back. There was only one person who had that deep of a voice and who would conveniently know where to find me. My feet hit pavement as I kept my car in sight, focusing on the dull gleam of the back window.

"Essallie, hold on." The voice said, the brush of air hitting my ear and neck. I turned to see Kayden keeping an even pace with me, face close enough to count the subtle freckles dusting his nose.

I leapt back and swore. "How the hell did you catch up to me?"

The delighted expression in his eyes melted as his shoulders slumped. "Really? Any question in the world you can ask a demon, and you ask how I caught up to you?"

I put out a hand to stop him. "Cut it with the demon crap. I hate when my brain plays games with me like this," I grumbled under my breath. "You're not a demon, you're either just a damn good projection of my imagination, or some kid who really does have too much time on his hands to have followed me all the way from New York."

He stopped walking and fell behind. I kept pushing forward and ignored the nagging need to look back over my shoulder.

Black smoke materialized in front of me, coiling into sharp wisps. Kayden stepped out from the lingering smoke, dusting off his shirt and flexing his hand as color bled back into his features. Within seconds he looked as normal and whole as I'd left him behind me moments before.

"How long are you going to fight this? Because really, I may have an eternity, but your skin's already starting to winkle and thin," he lamented with an expressionless face.

For a second I stood there in shock, mouth agape. Nervous words twisted in my mind, goose bumps rising high on my skin. "Smoke and mirrors, just smoke and mirrors." I swallowed hard, shoving past him to the car door. Sweat-slick hands fumbled inside my jacket for keys.

I heard him let out an infuriated sigh. "Essallie, this would go eons easier if you'd simply listen."

My messenger bag slipped off my shoulder, dropping to the ground with a thud. In one move I had turned around and locked eyes with him. He looked like he practically wanted to plead, beg on his hands and knees until the world crumbled around him. It only took one flashback to the leftovers of flesh and bone from Chase's body to plant me firmly back in the right frame of mind. I had to remember his motives weren't pure, that he was here to kill me, not help me. Death was his card to play.

"Go easier? Because death is *so* easy," I laughed darkly. "You're sick to think I'd even let you try to willingly kill me for one second."

He shook his head, eyebrows mashed together in concentration. "You've got it all wrong. I want to help you."

One pause was all it took. The question left my lips before I could ponder the consequences. "I don't understand. What do you mean?"

He came closer, shortening the distance between us by a few inches. One hand rested on the hood of my car. "Have you not been wondering what you really are?"

I reacted defensively. "Nothing's wrong with me."

"I never said anything was wrong." He looked like he ached to smile, but craftily masked it behind a look of emptiness. "You mean to tell me, you haven't been curious, not even a *teensy* bit?"

"What are you going on about?" I half-shouted back at him. My fists began to clench tight, warmth spreading out from my chest like it had the night before at the bonfire.

Kayden leaned in closer, his face centimeters from mine. He had no breath as he spoke, "I know what you are. Let me help."

Without thinking I gave him a push. Blue sparks of flame crackled under my fingertips, igniting a burst of fire on his clothes. Kayden stumbled back swearing and yelping. He smacked his chest like a mad man until the blaze was out.

I stood there, stunned. I looked down at my palms to see small kindling sparks dancing over the skin. Somehow it wasn't burning me. Somehow I was conducting fire. My head felt light, the world taking a curious spin onto an angle. I crashed into the side of my car, catching onto the side mirror and knocking it off with me.

My body shook as I spoke, scrambling to my feet and opening the car door. "You think you know me? You don't know a thing about me." I shoved my bag inside the car and got in, turning my neck to see Kayden standing several feet back. "There's nothing to find out, so stop. Leave me alone, Kayden, or I swear I'll-"

"You'll what? Kill me? You couldn't hurt a fly. If you had even an inch of how to control the power you have you wouldn't have hurt me even now."

"I don't have any power!" I screamed. Across the parking lot car alarms all went off at once. Headlights and taillights exploded and sparked uncontrollably. I shut the door and backed out, swerving the car until I could see Kayden.

Through the windshield I could barely make out his lips as they moved. I revved the engine. My threatening words from the night before came front and center in my mind, echoing with clarity.

"Go ahead and try," the whisper barely came out as I floored the car and sped past Kayden towards the only safe place I had left. My little House of Horror.

SIX
WICKED SOUL

Every day that followed the event in the parking lot, it started the same. Kayden would be waiting outside my locker, leaning against the wall with a silent expression of rage fit for a man about to murder everyone in sight. One look in my direction and the features softened, but only a little.

I opened my locker and shoved in everything for my afternoon classes, refusing to make eye contact with him. He was, after all, the one who put this on me. He brought every painful memory with him. A bug, ready to be squashed.

My locker slammed shut. I stared straight ahead, focusing on the little metal flaps. "What are you doing?"

"What does it look like I'm doing?" I didn't look to see. "I'm waiting, Essallie. Waiting for you to say you're curious, that you're ready. You know you only have to say the words, and you'll be that much closer to being rid of me for good." I felt his body shift closer, leaning into my stone posture. "So much for wanting a normal life, eh?"

I squared my shoulders tighter and turned, making sure to avoid even the faintest connection of our eyes. "Don't hold your breath, demon."

"Even if I wanted to, I'd be okay," he whispered, inching closer. "Demons don't need to breathe, you see. What about you, Essallie? Do you need to breathe?"

I bit my cheek. I wanted nothing better than to plunge my hands onto his chest and burn him back to wherever the hell he came from. His eyes were a shining obsidian when I stared back at him.

"Yes, Kayden, as a matter of fact I do. Humans need air for their lungs. You should know. Chase gasped for as much of it as he could when you used his skin to pick your teeth."

He shrugged. "Muscle gets wedged in there and flesh is the only thing I know to get it out. Sue me."

"You're impossible," I shook my head. "Nothing is going to change. Get used to the school system. You're going to need it if you plan on hanging around for the rest of my life." I walked past him, making sure not to touch the littlest bit of his body. If I wanted to start a fire I definitely didn't want to have it happen in a school.

Every day, despite repeated shutouts, Kayden remained persistent. He sat in every class, lingered around my locker like a lost creature, the Cafeteria, my car, you name it. Any chance he could to actively harass me into believing that I was something different, something not wholly human.

Sad truth was, part of me wanted to give into it. I had tried, and succeeded, in re-creating the fire in my room, bouncing a little ball of electric blue fire between my palms as if it were a regular bouncy ball. It felt like nothing, not hot or cold, but when it touched something it engulfed it whole until nothing was left.

One day after a particularly nasty screaming match in the hallway I was sure to be written up for, the rest of the day went like any other, and I moved from class to class with no interruption. Kayden had vanished, no doubt licking his wounds like the dog that he was. By the time I had made it to my car without a single sight of him, I was ecstatic. My words seemed to have finally sunk in. I went to bed grinning, feeling like I was going to have a better handle on everything, like my life was finally back on track.

My dreams that night were vivid, intensive. Long hallways with tall white pillars stretched on every side as I walked down an aisle. Grass blossomed beneath my feet, the sky above stretching to an everlasting horizon of melted purples and blues. It was a paradise, perfect in its own seclusion.

Tendrils of smoke curled behind me, licking up along the sides of my legs, twisting and trailing like slithering snakes. I ran forward, anything to avoid the smoke, for I knew if it took a hold of me it would be my end, my death. The pillars vanished under a dimming light, until suddenly I was standing at a precipice. Dirt escaped off the top of the edge, fumbling down into the endless darkness below. Somehow I knew falling into that abyss would be the same as giving into the smoke.

I spun around and fought back a gasp. The smoke had turned from small trails to a black mass, bubbling and growing, devouring all of the white light sanctuary left behind until nothing remained. It concentrated to one of my sides as the shape of a man stood beside me.

"This was all meant to be, Essallie," the smoke crooned as the two small flecks of light serving as eyes blinked with fluttered lashes. "Don't fight it. You were created for this." The smoke transformed into vines, sharp with thorns, and laced themselves around my ankles and legs, securing my wrists. It rushed over my skin in a thin cocoon until I was sealed off from the air. It pressed on my chest, forcing what was left of my air supply out until I had nothing.

I fought to move and scream, but my shallow attempt at a screech was lost under the folds of the dark matter. Fear ripped my insides as I thought of the possibility of dying. If you died in your sleep, did you die in real life?

Demons don't need to breathe, you see. What about you, Essallie? Do you need to breathe?

If I'd had any breath left I would have laughed. I had stopped moving and relaxed, letting the vines slice into my skin as they constricted tighter over my body. Heat flushed under my skin, fire curling inside my chest, a tiger waiting to strike. With the flip of a switch the fire spread like liquid lava through my skin, burning through my veins. I did nothing to hold it back as every pinprick with fresh blood ignited in a bright blue blaze, searing the vines off as if they were tissue paper.

The smoke-demon recoiled, bursts of red smoke exploding inside his chest and abdomen like a lightning storm in a summer sky. Horns spread from every inch of his body as he took solid shape, scales rippling his body. He lunged for me with outstretched hands coated in a shiny yellow liquid.

I dodged to the side just in time for him to scrape his hands on the ground. It instantly dissolved with a hiss and I knew it was acid. If it touched me I could kiss one of my limbs goodbye. I ran for the smoke, taking off into the darkness as far as I could run. An endless black stretched on every side, a satin curtain I couldn't find the end to. At some point I had to find a mark, a place to stop and hide. I was in the demon's playground now.

Laughter rippled through the darkness, echoing off every which way. I stopped, frantic, looking around for something, anything. But even the once grass below my feet had turned to a dull patch of dirt encrusted in dirty frost, leaving my feet frozen.

A wind picked up inside the dark, the force knocking me

down onto my feet. Something charged for me as screams stretched into the black, and without thinking I threw out my hand. The dazzling flame ignited over it, illuminating everything around me. Hundreds, thousands of demons of the twisted smoke lingered above me, reaching for me, their fingers covered in the same yellow liquid.

The fire reacted before I could, shooting twisted bolts at the demons, instantly incinerating them. The smoke dissipated into thin air, showing me I where I was. The sky and ground were the same muddy brown color, the only separating factor being the frost covering the ground. Lightning struck the sky, a jet black arc spiraling for me. At the front of the lighting was the first demon I had seen, his face melting into the smoke with a final laugh.

The arc blew through my chest, knocking me to the ground as the fire in my hand died. Pain rattled my bones as I felt everything inside of me dying one by one. My body stopped moving, eyes shutting. I watched in horror as the demon came forward and leaned over, the long grin on his face revealing an endless supply of flesh-ripping teeth.

"And so it begins," he said just as he plunged his hand into my chest.

I woke up in a jolt, screaming as loud as I could. Everything around me was dark, too dark for comfort. I scrambled out of bed and smacked into my end table as I flipped on my bedroom light. Nothing but my own four walls, small assortment of sketch books and piles of dirty laundry. A pounding on the door made me jump and hit my end table again.

"Essallie, you okay? What the hell was that?" I opened the door to find Jayson standing there in a t-shirt, pajama pants, and a baseball bat in one hand. He looked flabbergasted when I started laughing.

"So, were you planning on using that at all?" I managed

between laughs.

He did his best not to glare. "You never know, some of the boys in this town are rowdy as hell."

I put my hands to my ears and shook my head hard. "Oh no, nuh-uh, you are not saying this stuff in front of me. Goodnight Jayson." I pushed him towards the door but he stopped me. His face was pulled down into a sharp frown.

"What is that?" He pointed to my bed. I turned to where he had pointed and dropped my hands when I saw it. There were burnt marks on my sheets and comforter. I felt myself turn to ice. My mind spun and I sputtered the first lie that popped into my head.

"Oh, whoops. My crayons for art class must have gotten on there the other night while I was sketching." I pushed him back outside the door. "Don't worry about it, I'll do the laundry tomorrow."

"But-"

"Goodnight, Jayson," I said and shut the door in his face. As soon as I was sure he wasn't standing in front of my door did the hysterical breathing begin. Great, I was now conjuring fire in my sleep.

I pressed my back against the door and tried to even my breathing as I thought. It couldn't have been me, there was no physical way a human could create fire without matches, with gasoline, sticks, stones, whatever. You didn't just snap your fingers and create a mini ball of flame in your hands.

Raising a shaking arm out in front of me, I held my hand out and snapped my fingers. Twisted blue flame instantly ran over my fingers and hand until the whole thing was engulfed. I shook my hand and put the fire out, fighting not to scream or cry. The mirror across my room showed me, only what looked back didn't look like a scared little girl anymore. It looked like a person hiding an ugly truth. A person who wasn't human.

SEVEN
THROUGH THE FLAMES

The week following my bizarre nightmare and setting the sheets on fire, my patience had been growing thin. Kayden had resorted to escorting me to every class, the same bitterly-twisted smile on his face that reminded me of the winter wonderland that was forming outside. Snow had been falling on and off for days, but the predictions had said in less than a week we'd be hit with a blizzard beyond all blizzards, calling for over five feet of pure sparkling white fluff.

Sitting at the lunch table and talking to Abigail, I caught a glimpse of flurries melting against the large pane window.

"So they said Jessica's still in Portland?" I had asked Abigail. A forkful of lettuce sat on top a plate filled with the leafy greens mostly abandoned. Sadly, it was the only thing I could stomach these days.

Between mouthfuls of chicken parmesan, she nodded. "Tests said she has a tumor, but it's weird. One day it's there, the next it's not. They've been re-running the same tests over and over to confirm it really is there before they do surgery."

I shook my head. How insane. I went to speak when Kayden interrupted. "Sounds like a flickering miracle. Maybe she could use a little help." He pointedly turned to face me. His eyes were different today, a shining chocolate brown that reminded me of my favorite candy bar commercial.

"Maybe a fundraiser?" Emily suggested, but Kayden shook his head.

"Essallie would know how," he said.

"Sorry, I'm busy curing Diabetes this week," I rolled my eyes and leaned back in my chair for a moment before standing and grabbing my things. "Excuse me."

"You forgot your tray," Abigail pointed out.

"Let Kayden get it, since he thinks he knows everything about me, he might as well just take my place." I left the table before anyone could catch up to me, getting to my classroom in record time. The door was locked, the inside dark with empty desks. No one would be back for an easy ten minutes.

Behind me there was a guttural noise. A deep throated cough that sounded a lot like-

I sighed. "How nice of you to join me."

"I'm only trying to help."

Spinning sharp on my feet I came face to face with Kayden. The white t-shirt he wore was covered in spirals of varying colors that left me dizzy if I stared at it too long. Between here and the Cafeteria his eyes had changed to a liquid blue that danced with every move of his face. All of him was a charm today, no doubt meant to make me give into his little game. I was furious. Who was he to think that by looking appealing I'd simply give into his whim? Rage blossomed in my chest like a flower in full bloom, the heat instantly extending to my fingertips and palms.

"Help? You're trying to help? Let me tell you just what you can do to *help*," I hissed. I pressed a hand into his chest, blue fire automatically jumping from my skin and racing over his clothes. The fire wrapped around his frame like rope binding a body to a tree.

His eyes bled back to the shining black onyx I had seen the first night we met. "It's eating you alive, you're drowning in the power."

Every hair on my body rose. The veins in my arms pulsed faster and faster as a warming rush of adrenaline spilled over my body. "To help me, you can leave. Or I will make you. Make your choice, demon. Fire or life."

The fire was growing, spreading past the bands that held him in place. Tiny rivulets raced over his face and burned into his cheeks and hair. "It will kill you, you know," he hissed under the burn of the fire. "If you don't get help in time there will be nothing left. You'll burn from the inside out. Your own blood betraying you."

My grasp on the fire weakened, the flames flickering and receding. He was bluffing, he had to be. Kayden burst outward into black smoke, returning to his human shape across the hall, away from my grasp.

The fire crackled inside my palms, slowly dulling to nothing. As soon as the flames died my knees gave out. My entire body shook and I struggled to breathe. Sweat coated every inch of my skin, leaving me feel like I had just dipped into a bucket of ice water.

Kayden came closer but still hung back. His expression was guarded. "It's already burning you out. Don't you feel it? Like the air will never return to your lungs?"

Slowly I slid down the lockers until I was sitting against them, gasping for breath. The room was spinning into one giant pile of color. I shook my head and blinked, trying to re-set my eyes before I passed out, or worse, threw up from the spinning sensation. "I don't need your help."

Amidst the colors came a laugh. "Of course you don't."

"Just because I'm passing out on the floor doesn't mean I

can't still detect sarcasm you twit."

My eyes started to re-focus, the blurry image of Kayden kneeling before me came into view first. "You need help. Before you lose control and hurt someone."

"Like you?" I snapped. I tried to stand but slipped back down to the floor from jelly legs. "I don't know what this, this thing is, but I'm not going to let it ruin my life. You've already done enough of that for me." Another attempt to stand failed and I found myself back on the floor shaking. With one final push I stood tall, staring down Kayden as he continued to kneel.

"Stay there, I like you better when you're bowing at my feet," I whispered as a throng of students came up into the hallway. Our teacher came down the hall and opened the door for class.

English was one of the few subjects I had no problem tuning into and focusing in. Kayden was seated out of my sight, Abigail right next to me, and anything the teacher liked to dish was relatively easy for me to handle, especially when I had already read all of Shakespeare's works in 6th grade out of sheer boredom.

"We're going to continue with our look into *Othello* today, so open your tombstones under your desks," the teacher muttered darkly. It was a never-ending joke with her class that she called the textbooks tombstones since they practically weighed as much as one.

As I reached underneath for my copy of the book I felt a stab in my stomach. Automatically I sat up straight and breathed, the hot-knife feeling only growing worse.

"You okay?" Abigail raised her eyebrows at me. I gave her a little nod and slowly reached back down for the book under my chair. Another stab sharper than the last hit my stomach again, the pain spreading into my chest with a burning sensation I'd never felt before. I doubled over and pressed my forehead to the cool desktop.

From the back of the classroom I heard Kayden. "Essallie doesn't look too good."

The teacher took one look at me and panicked. "Oh no no no, I am not having another kid get sick in my class. Abigail, take her down to the nurse, quickly."

An arm slipped around my shoulders and hoisted me out of my seat. It was all I could do to keep my lips pressed tight from screaming at the pain. "Get her things. She's on fire, I can feel the fever coming off of her in waves."

Wait, that was Kayden talking, not Abigail. Kayden was the one carrying me out of the classroom, and into the hall, and down to the nurse. I wanted to spit in his face, maybe even set him on fire in front of everyone for a little show. I was getting sick of him trying to play hero to my slips and falls.

Eyes closed, I felt him carry me out of the classroom and down the hallway, Abigail right by my side. "She was fine this morning," I heard her say. "Hell she was fine two minutes ago. What do you think happened?"

"My theory probably isn't the one you want to hear," Kayden replied truthfully. He lightly adjusted his arms to hold me up better. "She wouldn't like me to spread my ideas."

Too true. Letting everyone know I could potentially engulf them in flames if they looked at me crossways would probably put a damper on my mood. "What, do you think she brought something with her from New York? Like a Typhoid Mary of the modern era? Bad ass."

"Not quite, but sure, we can go with that," Kayden laughed.

"I'm right here, you know," I whispered through tight lips. Pain was driving down into my bones, stabbing like millions of scalded, jagged blades into my skin. He turned into the infirmary and followed the nurse's directions to set me down on a cot in the back room while Abigail explained everything in the other room.

"It's happening, you know," he whispered in a low tone.

"Nothing is happening," I managed to snap back at him. "It's just a reaction to lunch. I haven't been handling food well. Must be coming down with a bug."

He shook his head. "If she takes your temperature, it's going to show you should be dead. Your powers are coming in, like it or not. What happens next is how you handle it."

I raised my head off the pillow as much as I could manage. "How about I just set you on fire and get it over with?"

"I hope you're still this feisty when the fever wears off," Kayden said, the corners of his lips twitching.

"You haven't seen a fraction of it yet," I laughed despite myself and let my head back down onto the pillow. Sweat beaded and trickled over my skin, suctioning the pillow and flimsy sheets to me like glue.

The nurse stepped in with Abigail and immediately shooed Kayden away from me. Both hung back as she ran one of the new thermometers over my forehead and waited for the reading. When the results came up she shook her head and reset it before running it over my head again. But the results left her face just as ashen as it had the first time.

"Can't be right," she smacked the device in her hands a couple of times. "Let me try again before I get the old one."

"What did it say?" I asked in spite of myself.

She laughed, nervously almost. "This new technology is so temperamental. It said you have a fever of 120 degrees, but there's just no way that's possible. You'd be dead." The reading flashed at her again and she jammed it into her pocket. "Now it's saying 122 degrees. I'm getting the old one."

I felt my stomach drop, the pain flaring through my body again. She turned around and sent both Abigail and Kayden back to class but not before I had a chance to steal a look at Kayden. His eyes were shining like polished coal, his lips curved into a tight-lipped smile.

After seven different attempts with both the old and new thermometers the nurse finally called Jayson to pick me up and take me home for the day. She stressed that ice baths, ice packs and cool rags would surely bring the fever down and break it within the day. He led me up to my room and made sure to bring rags in every half hour soaked in borderline frozen water. Nothing was bringing the fever down.

Between hazes of the fever and pain that forced me into blackouts I had fitful dreams. Creatures of all shapes and sizes continued to reach out to me as I used the fire to burn them past my path. By the time I would wake up the fever would be spiking higher, the pain so intense I'd throw up.

At one point I managed to drag myself to the tub and turn on the faucets, shoving myself in with my clothes still on. The water felt worse than the stabbing pain inside me, and I screamed. Jayson had run upstairs to pull me from the water and back to my bed, but he said my fever seemed to have gone down from the bath.

I felt like I was dying. Nothing wanted to work, from my legs to my heart, it all moved like an animal on its last leg. Each breath felt like I was putting all of my energy into it. Giving in suddenly seemed easier, plausible.

Jayson knocked on the door, startling me from my haze of thought. "I need to run out for a few hours. Are you going to be okay?"

Slowly I nodded. "Sleeping it off," I said.

He brought my cell phone over to the bed and rested it under my hand. "Just dial if it gets any worse and I'll be home in a heartbeat. I'll make sure to pick up more ice on the way home." He closed the door behind him. I gave into the waves of pain I'd been fighting back and fell into a dreamless sleep.

Sometime in the night I startled awake. My bedroom light had been left on, a bucket by the side of the bed, rags piled onto my nightstand. Curiously I didn't feel like I had a fever and the pain inside my body had vanished. Slowly I rose out of bed, ungluing myself from the sheets that had been soaked in water and sweat. I had only one thing in mind; water.

I tip-toed past Jayson's room in case he was asleep, down the steps and to the kitchen. My favorite cup I brought from home, a Jack Skellington mug, sat in the drainer with a couple other plates and silverware. I filled it with a little tap water and took my time sipping it, gazing out the window above the kitchen sink.

The cup half-slipped from my hands as I spotted a figure standing in the backyard. Against the glassy night the silhouette seemed almost impossible to spot. I reached for the baseball bat under the sink when I stopped and stared at my hand.

I opened the door and stepped outside in the still-soaked clothes I'd been wearing earlier, but the air felt soft and almost warm on my skin. Small snowflakes hung in the air, leaving little trails as they fluttered to the ground. My feet stepped onto the frost covered ground as I walked slowly, hands at each side ready to strike. The figure never moved, only stared straight at me as I came closer.

"Get off my property before I call the police," I warned the figure. I stopped walking to leave a small chunk of distance between us. "You won't get a second warning."

"What if I want a second warning?" The voice asked as the figure smirked, gleaming white teeth revealing themselves.

"You have got to be freaking kidding me," I swore aloud as my eyes adjusted to the dark, painting Kayden into my sight. He still had the same clothes on from school, still the same short spiky black hair, and still the same ridiculous smirk on his face I wanted to cut off with nail clippers. "*Kayden what the hell are you doing on my lawn?"*

"Waiting for you, what else am I supposed to do?" He shrugged and came over to me, tilting his head on one side. "Still feeling like you're on death's door?"

"In the middle of the night no less!" I screamed louder and threw my hands into the air. "You've got more than just a few issues here, you know that right? There's just no way I can't explain this to my brother in the morning."

"Brother?" He questioned, and I nodded. "Huh. Weird. Warlocks usually only adopt one child."

"What?"

"Nothing, never mind, never mind." He puffed out his cheeks for a moment. "So, are you ready to finally accept it?"

I rolled my eyes and sighed despite myself. "Really, Kayden? I feel like I nearly die and the only thing you want to know is if I'm ready for your little game still? You get old fast." I turned around and started the walk back to my house. Kayden caught up and fell in silently by my side.

"And here I thought maybe feeling your insides burn up would make you curious about the new unbridled power running rampant through your veins, but hey, that's just me," he said sharply.

I turned to say something to him when I tripped and fell onto the ground. A sharp pain shot up my right elbow as I felt the skin scratch itself apart. I got back up to my feet easily and took a look at my elbow. Fresh blood bubbled out of the scrapped skin staining the skin and my sleeve.

"Go figure I spend a whole day convulsing to death and don't have a scratch on me, but then I step outside and manage to hurt myself around you," I grumbled stiffly under my breath. I turned to look up at Kayden but he vanished into thin air. "Kayden?"

The air around me rippled and before I knew it something was hurtling towards me. I crossed my arms and covered my face before screaming. The rippling grew with force then suddenly stopped just as a burst of bright light illuminated the backyard.

I waited for whatever was going to hit me, only it never came. I opened my eyes slowly and moved my arms down, but I definitely wasn't ready for what I saw.

The entire backyard was cast in a soft, angelic white light. Kayden stood across from me, his face contorted and twisted with the horns and scales of the face I had first seen. His mouth was open and growling, showing his razor-sharp teeth. Only his eyes held the tiniest shred of humanity as they bled a color of melted gold through the onyx. He didn't step closer to me or make a move, but his eyes stared all around me as if something was right beside me. That's when I saw them.

Two long, see-through crystal wings arched around me, their shimmering glamour eerily hypnotic. Both wings spread out, spanning nearly the whole backyard. It was then I realized that they were what had protected me from whatever had tried to attack me. I wanted to thank the creature, the angel that had saved me, but when I turned around I saw no one. I spun back to look at Kayden who still stood unmoving across the yard, a knowing smile spread sickeningly wide across his face. Carefully I reached behind my back and stopped in horror as I felt the extension of something from my back. The wings were mine.

My eyes rolled into my head and I blacked out.

EIGHT
A FLUTTER OF CRYSTAL

Cold. Everything was cold. I couldn't shake the feeling I was under water. My skin felt wet, slick with the chilling liquid that rolled over me in swallowing waves.

Another wave hit. "Wakey wakey, Ess-uh-lee."

My eyes snapped open and came into view. Kayden held a bucket just above my head, water dripping from the rim. Well, at least explained why I was soaking wet.

I sat up slowly, shivering from the breeze I created with each move. My clothes and hair were soaked to the bone as if I had jumped into the ocean for a midnight swim.

"How long was I out?"

He sat down across from me and tossed the bucket to the side. Within second it had disintegrated into nothing, as if it had never even existed. "Three, five minutes maybe?"

I nodded absentmindedly as I started to wring out my hair as best my frozen, shaking hands could do. When our eyes met, the question quietly slipped out of my lips. "What just happened, Kayden?"

The smug smile I had seen only minutes ago turned thoughtful, almost pensive. "Are you saying you're finally admitting to there being something off?"

My eyes drifted down to ends of my hair. Admitting something was off would mean he was right. Admitting something was off would mean I believed everything I had just seen and felt for the last few days. The fire, the emotions, the wings. Was it all real or was he just playing a trick on my mind?

I looked back at Kayden. "What am I?"

The smallest of smiles touched his lips, but his eyes were shining. Swirls of obsidian and slate weaved in his eyes. "You should get inside before you get sick. Magical or not, you can still get a cold."

I nodded and stood up, shaking my arms of the excess water drops that clung to my skin. Everything felt so surreal, so fake, as if any moment I would wake up and find myself still in bed shaking from a broken fever and clinging to drenched sheets.

Kayden followed me inside the house and handed me a ripped sheet of paper towels to dry off with. I collapsed onto the nearest chair in the kitchen and took them. My face pressed in them I made sure to hide the small prickle of tears that melded in with the water from my face. This was all real. I couldn't pretend it was accident or coincidence anymore.

I looked over to Kayden as he leaned against the marble countertops, his fingers absentmindedly playing with one of the drawer handles. He seemed just as lost as I felt right now.

"Your kind hasn't existed for almost three hundred years." His head tilted to face the ceiling. "Funny, I had been thinking this whole time you were some kind of warlock or under the protection of one." He shook his head. "Oh how wrong I was."

"What does that mean? What am I, Kayden?"

He didn't turn to look down at me. "You have many names, but the most common is Nephilim."

"I don't know what that means," I brought the paper towel off my face. My hands rested in my lap and twisted the damp towel over and over. "I don't know what any of this means."

"It means you're a hybrid. Half-human, half-angel." He leaned off of the counter and pulled out a chair from the table. Slumping into it backwards he continued. "You're the stuff of legend. The thing demons would tell their children to scare them straight. Warlock spells I can handle, warlocks I can handle. Vampires, faeries, werewolves, other demons I all know and can handle. But this, I don't even know what to do."

We sat there in silence as I tried to wrap the words around my head. Half-human, half-angel, he had said. My heart warmed just at the thought of it, a curious sensation of heat spreading through every extension of my body.

"We have to play this carefully," Kayden said out of the blue. I looked up to find him staring at me intently. "If anyone were to find out-"

"Who could I possibly tell?" I asked sarcastically. "Like my brother would even believe me if I did. Or Abigail for that matter. Actually, she would, you know, after she'd dial the nearest psych ward."

He frowned. "I'm serious, Essallie. This can't go past the two of us until I figure out where to go from here." His eyes glazed over for a second to a thoughtful faraway stare. "There has to be a reason for this. Nephilim don't just pop up out of the blue."

"This isn't your problem, Kayden, stop treating it like it is. Everything will work out." I snapped at him. He wasn't the one who had to suddenly deal with the problem of setting things on fire. He didn't have to deal with wings sprouting from his back, at least I didn't think so. I stood up from my chair the same time he did. "Have you really been alive for over three hundred years?"

Pushing his chair in, he nodded absentmindedly. "Longer than your pretty little mind can wrap around. You're right, everything will work out. I'll see if I can find anything in some of the books I have at home." His lips twisted. "I won't count on it, though, unless you think stories of an ancient mythical being would exist in the fine print of a Playboy?"

I made a face just as my eyes spotted the clock hanging above the door frame. "You should go. Last thing I need is my brother catching a boy in the house in the middle of the night."

"Personally, I wouldn't really call myself a *boy*," he drawled with a mischievous smile on his face. "I'm sure he didn't mention anything about finding a demon in your room now, did he?"

"As a matter of fact, I think he did," I replied and smacked his arm. The effect was like striking flint; fire marked where I touched him and spiraled into the air, dying before it hit the ground. Kayden's arm vanished off in a trail of tasteless smoke. It reappeared in an instant, unscathed as if I'd never touched him.

"How do you-" I started when I saw headlights beam through the house. Jayson. My eyes nearly bulged out of my head. "He's home, get out of here." When I didn't hear the door open I turned around to burn him out if I had to, only I was alone. "Thanks for the goodbye."

The air to my left swirled into a makeshift silhouette of a head and shoulders. "You said to leave. Or would you like me to meet your fleshy blood sibling?"

I heard the front door open, feet lumbering inside. "No! Go!" My voice cracked and threatened to burst as I tried to keep it low.

"Essallie?" Jayson's voice carried down the hallway as I watched the light turn on. He stepped into the kitchen and flicked on the light as I stood there. "What are you doing down here in the dark?"

I held out the paper towel I still had in my hands. For the most part it had been reduced to a twisted and shredded mess. "It was a little cooler down here with the lights off."

He set down two large bags of ice onto the table and came over to me. His hand pressed against my forehead for a minute. "I think your fever broke. That's good. Any longer and I would have had to drive you to Portland."

Too bad a hospital would have done jack-crap for me. Unless they had a manual on mythical hybrids and weird people. "I'm actually feeling pretty good right now. Tired, but good." I stretched out toward the ceiling and yawned.

"Then get back to bed. Don't push it just in case," Jayson said and turned me toward the hallway for the stairs. "I'm just glad you didn't have those hallucinations like you did when we were kids."

I'd made it halfway down the hallway when I stopped and looked over my shoulder. "What hallucinations?"

Jayson leaned against the doorframe and shrugged, running his hands through his hair. "You were just a kid but you used to swear you saw angels." He let out a soft chuckle as he reminisced. "You even went as far to tell us you saw Dad."

My throat felt drier than a desert. Tears stung my eyes as I made sure to keep every ounce of emotion out of my voice. If only Jayson knew just how close to the truth he was.

"Some imagination."

NINE
TRADING ENEMY LINES

Saturday morning was greeted with snow, and tons of it. The news had talked about only a foot or two at the most but we ended up with a staggering six feet of pure white fluff. One look in the backyard told me I wouldn't be seeing anything green and leafy for a long, long time.

I had stepped downstairs when I heard more than one voice in the kitchen. Jayson was laughing at something over the sound of sizzling and scraping of pans.

I poked my head tentatively into the kitchen and nearly screamed in surprise. Kayden was sitting at the table dressed in a heavy snow jacket, snow pants and boots, chomping down on a plate of scrambled eggs coated in ketchup and pepper. Jayson had his own plate set at the table next to a large pitcher of steaming coffee, two strips of meat cooking in the pan he was standing alongside.

Kayden spotted me first. "Hey, look who's feeling better. Jayson told me you were still asleep upstairs."

Jayson grinned at me over his shoulder. "It's alive! You

hungry?" He held the pan out to me, the strips of meat smelling downright revolting. I wrinkled my nose and shook my head as I willed myself not to vomit.

Sitting down, Kayden shoveled another forkful of eggs into his mouth. "What's the matter?"

I glared darkly at the back of Jayson's head. "Jayson knows I don't like fish. It smells worse than dirty gym socks and spoiled food and-"

"Entrails and coffins and stomach acid?" He offered.

Jayson let out a loud burst of laughter. "He's been making jokes like that all morning! Between shoveling the driveway and door out of that crap. Why didn't you tell me about your little friend, Essie?"

I made sure Jayson was focused on cooking his putrid breakfast before I spoke to Kayden in a hushed tone. "What the hell are you doing here?"

"Care for some eggs?" He asked aloud, holding a forkful out to me. "How'd you sleep?"

"Like an angel."

"Oh the irony," he fought to keep his face straight between chews.

I reached out to smack his hand but stopped. My fingers hovered dangerously close to his, small sparks clicking at my fingertips. He raised an eyebrow at me, watching to see what I would do. Would I really start something with Jayson only a few feet away from us? I pulled the plate of eggs across the table instead, taking the fork Jayson had laid out for himself and took a bite.

"You still didn't answer my question, demon," I whispered. "Why are you here?"

"Always with the questions," he mocked me with crossed eyes and puffed out cheeks. "What have I been saying from the beginning? I'm here to help you."

"Maybe I don't want your help. Ever think of that?" I

took another bite from his plate.

"I think you need me more than you realize right now."

"I think you're full of bullshit."

"Was that a quivering lip I saw? Shiver of the shoulders?"

I set my fork down and fought to control the itching sensation in my palms. If I didn't keep my temper in check the table would pay for it. "You're lucky my brother's in here or you'd be reduced to ashes right now."

"Now is that any way to treat a guest?"

"Someone say brother?" Jayson said out of the blue, bringing the pan over to the table. He looked at Kayden's empty plate in front of me in horror. "Essie I hope you didn't eat any of that."

His tone made me nervous. I stared at the plate and back at Kayden. "Why?"

"Kayden had salmon chopped in those eggs." He looked at Kayden while he scooped his own strips of the pink meat onto his plate. "You didn't tell her?"

He shrugged but I caught the smirk he fought to keep off his face. "She said she didn't need my help." He looked at me. "Sorry, Essie."

My stomach felt uncomfortable. I tried to keep the image of dead fish out of my head as I stood up from the table. "You know what? I'm going to go get dressed and help with the shoveling outside."

Jayson shook his head and swallowed whatever he had eaten off his plate. "We already took care of it this morning. Kayden said one of your friends could use a little help in town though. Abigail, I think?"

"Okay, sounds good. I'll be ready in five," I nodded and headed upstairs. Down the hallway I heard Jayson say, "That means you might as well sit tight for another half hour." Boys. I bit my tongue and started up the steps, making a mental note to let everyone know Jayson still sings in the shower higher than Michael Jackson when the time was right.

Stumbling down the steps in the boots and snowsuit I'd brought before moving to Maine I met Kayden at the bottom of the steps a couple of minutes later. The original plan had been that I would hide inside for all the freakish weather. I hadn't actually planned on using any of it.

We walked outside, Jayson helping me most of the way so I didn't slip and roll downhill. Kayden's jet black Hummer sat at the bottom of our driveway, virtually brand new. I bet he hadn't even put on a hundred miles on it yet. Once inside the car Jayson waved us off as we turned off the road and made our way into town.

"So, five minutes, eh?" Kayden snickered as he kept his eyes on the road. I punched him on the shoulder, fire exploding from the contact. He only sighed and let his arm vanish into nothing before reforming back to its original form.

"If you couldn't do that smoke-thing I don't think there'd be anything left of you by now," I said thoughtfully, staring out the window as he drove slower than a snail down the main road. Almost everyone was outside helping one another shovel out doorways and windows. Small barrels of fire lined down the road every few feet. A sudden thought dawned upon me and I turned to Kayden. "We're not really going to Abigail's, are we?"

He pursed his lips and adjusted his grip on the steering wheel ever so slightly. "You're really not going to like me after this."

"Are you kidnapping me?" I asked hesitantly. If he said yes, I had a feeling jumping from the car and running home would leave me with minor injuries.

Thankfully he laughed. "Do you think I would have spent all that time getting to know your brother if I was planning on kidnapping you? Please." He made a turn and headed down the road before making a sharp right into the development

Leo lived in. "Don't worry, we won't be alone if that's what you're afraid of."

He brought the car to a stop inside a driveway, came over to my door and did his best to help me out without touching each other. With both feet on solid ground I looked up to the mansion in front of us. The brick-and-mortar build reminded me of a colonial set decor, from the white shutters to the marble steps and porch leading to the large dark wood double doors carved with minimal detailing. It looked oddly whimsical, as if someone didn't want to leave the past behind.

Kayden and I walked up the steps, thankful someone had already shoveled off the mass of snow and laid salt down to prevent any ice. He knocked on the door a few times using the brass knocker and hung back to wait.

One of the doors swung open. Ursula stood in the entrance, in all of her ethereal beauty, dressed in a t-shirt and shorts and knee-length socks running up her toothpick thin legs. Her already narrow eyes thinned to slits as she pursed her lips. She gave Kayden and I the most profoundly withering look I'd ever seen anyone do.

"Oh hell no," she finally said, and moved to close the door.

Kayden shoved his foot between the door and the frame. One arm rested on the polished wood as he leaned inside the frame to the house. "Be a doll and let us in, won't you?"

Her eyes locked on me over Kayden's shoulder. "And why in the hell should I do that?"

"Must we go over all these formalities, Ursula?"

She looked from me to Kayden, jaw locked. The tension was almost too much to bear until she finally caved. "Fine."

Kayden ushered me inside, pressing a finger to his lips when our eyes met. I nodded, but I still had no clue as to why of all the places he chose to take me to it was Ursula's house. The girl practically wanted me six feet under just for the benefit of dancing on my grave.

The door shut, she spun around still sporting the withering look on her face. "My father's going to hear about this."

"Same excuse different day?" Kayden drawled, rolling his eyes as he walked onto their carpet with his dirty shoes. "That man's your father the way you're the Queen of England."

"I beg your pardon?" She stepped closer, eyes burning with a look of pure hatred. "Don't you dare insult my father-"

"No way in hell that mortal is your father, Ursula," Kayden spat right back but his tone remained eerily calm. "Give up the game. Why else would I be here?"

Her expression turned from hatred to despair in one heartbeat. "You said never again, Kayden. You swore! Last time you ousted me I nearly died."

"I told you that was an accident. I hadn't meant to point you as a witch in the Salem trials, it was supposed to be Annie. Water under the bridge."

"Don't you mean water over my head? They tried drowning me you idiot. I had to fake my own death for three days!"

"At least you're pale enough to actually fake it. Imagine if you had color in your cheeks like you did in Rome."

"That was blood, not blush. Timothy's blood, to be exact. That stuff lasted forever bottled."

I watched their exchange with confusion. Ursula wasn't human, obviously, if she had been alive during the Salem Witch Trials and still looked like she was sixteen. "Wait a minute, what the hell are you?" Kayden and Ursula stopped talking and looked at me. Apparently I had been forgotten in their reminiscing.

"What is she doing here?" Ursula asked in a low tone.

Kayden shook his head as he removed his snow suit. "She's fine, trust me. Essie has a few secrets of her own, that's why we're here."

I didn't feel comfortable with this. My palms began to itch as I shook my head. "I don't understand, is she a demon too?"

He busted out laughing and came over to pat my shoulder but stopped and pulled his hand back slowly. "She only wishes she was a demon. At least she wouldn't have to eat anyone then. Ursula's one of the prettier succubi I've had the pleasure of meeting in my ever-lasting existence."

My eyes widened and I stared at Ursula. It made so much more sense now why she went through boyfriends like she owned shoes. But one thing didn't make sense. "Hold up, you said eat. I don't remember there being any murder investigations or missing students in our school."

She gave a dainty little shrug with a small smile. "I don't have to be dating them to feed on them, honey. Flesh is flesh." She examined her nails with minimal interest. "I'm trying to reform myself and not kill the humans I fall in love with. It makes for a much better relationship down the road."

"Still wish you could say that with your boy-toy back in the '20s, don't you?" Kayden laughed darkly. He took Ursula's outstretched arm and spun her into himself before leaning her back in a sweeping move you'd see on a ballroom dance floor.

Her face briefly flashed to a look of anger. Pulling back from him and brushing her arms she muttered something under her breath about mistakes and hunger. "Why now Kayden?"

"Long story, trust me," he said. "We need to use your library."

"Down the hall and to the right," Ursula said without pause.

Kayden shook his head. "No, I mean the other library."

She sized him up for a minute, her face twisted between laughter and surprise. "You can't access that. It's been barred to others for the last few hundred years."

"Right along the time Alexandria was lost to the fire, I know. We need to see it. There's a chance one of those tombs will hold what we need."

"What exactly is it you need, Kayden?"

"Can't tell you that."

His harshness took her back. Ursula's eyebrows slowly rose and something flickered in her eyes. Her pupils grew until all color vanished from her eyes, and when she smiled I noticed her teeth had turned from perfect squares to thin spikes as white as snow.

She sauntered forward, her hips swaying in a hypnotic trance I found hard to look away from. "But you can, Kayden." She cooed with the rhythm of a sweet lullaby. "You can tell me anything. Don't you want to share your little secret with me?"

I stood there in a trance as she danced closer to his body, each step thinning the gap between them. She stopped in front of him and slowly arched her chest into his, curving into him like a python wrapping around its prey. I watched as she slid her hands one at a time under his shirt, exposing his bare skin.

A bright blue burst of flames temporarily blinded all three of us. My hand reached out somewhere just as Ursula let out a blood-curling scream. As the light faded I found Kayden was pressed on top of Ursula, shielding her. The skin on her arm had burns in the pattern of ribbons racing over her arm, the ribbon effect matching on Kayden's arm as well. I looked down to my hands to see the remnants of fire still resting on my fingertips, as if it were waiting for a second round.

He sighed and stood up, folding his arms over his chest. He looked over to me and shook his head.

"Way to let the cat out of the bag, Essie."

"I didn't mean to," I gasped and shook my hands

vigorously until the flames vanished. "I don't know what happened. One second she was talking to you and the next the whole room went white." I turned to Ursula, who remarkably hadn't said a word. "I am so sorry Ursula, really I didn't mean to."

Kayden helped Ursula up from the ground. He examined the burn on her arm, blood pressing through the charred skin as the remaining skin started to turn red and swell. He leaned in and whispered into her ear, running his fingers over the wound. The edges began to grow inward, shrinking the wound until nothing was left. Her skin looked perfect and untouched.

"Not even a scar," Kayden said aloud, stepping back from Ursula. "Now, the library?"

Ursula nodded and led the way. We came to a small study office where she flipped a light switch to open a wall that led down a series of steps lined in crimson carpet and fake torches. The staircase winded down to what looked initially like a large wine cellar until the lights came on. Bookshelves packed to the brim lined every wall and filled every nook and cranny. Aisles stretched on forever, standing bookshelves creating and endless sea of rows that held no end. Every so often a chair would be randomly placed in front of the end of an aisle, books clustered around the feet of the chair and on the cushions.

Kayden and Ursula seemed completely unimpressed. I however couldn't stop staring. It was hard to not appreciate the mass of the collection that had to have taken them hundreds of years easily.

"Careful with the ones on the red shelf, they require a blood payment to read them," Ursula said over her shoulder. A thin smile stretched on her lips as she touched her neck. I spotted a small butterfly shaped scar I had never seen there before. Maybe she spoke from experience. I wondered how much she had to sacrifice to get what she wanted in the end.

Kayden walked down the aisles slowly, scanning up and down. He finally settled on a small blue leather-bound book with a detailed gold leafing. Unlike most of the musty texts around it this one looked virtually untouched, as perfect as the day the creator finished it.

He set the book down on the nearest table and beckoned us closer. Opening it to the middle he began to flip around through the pages. Every couple of pages I saw drawings illustrating people with wings drawn inside a ball of blue fire.

"Why would you have a library of the supernatural in your basement?" I looked at Ursula out of the corner of my eyes.

She didn't meet my gaze. "It belonged to my other half." She sniffed and made a face. "He was the academic out of us both. First it was just a few books, next thing you knew it was every book on spells and blood curses and creatures."

"What happened to him?"

"He died as all mortals do," she replied dryly, still refusing to meet my stare. I felt my cheeks start to burn, an apology on my tongue when Kayden shushed at us both.

Pointing to a part in the book he frowned. "This whole damn book is in scripture." He looked at Ursula. "Do you have the key?"

"Somewhere in here, I think," she said slowly, biting her lower lip. "I don't know where, though."

"You mean to tell me you don't have all of this in a computer for reference?"

"Be my guest," she snapped. "I still only have 24 hours in a day to get things done, immortal or not."

They both began to bicker, arguing over keeping up appearances for humans. I stared at the page Kayden had left open. A small picture in the top right showed two people, one of them extending a book to the other. The one with wings, an angel I presumed, accepted the book.

"It doesn't look like scripture to me," I said aloud. Both stopped arguing and turned to look at me. "I can read it just fine." I understood the scribbles on the pages perfectly, as if I had known it all along.

"What?" Kayden paused for a moment before smacking his head. A huge grin spread across his face. "Of course you can read it. Don't know why I didn't think to ask you first. Well, what does it say?"

I started at the top of the page and worked my way down. The aged paper crinkled under my touch. "'Their bodies are not temples like their creators, but prisons of fire and destruction. Once they come into age they ignite the matches of war against all of the unholy and inhuman, leaving none safe in their path.'"

I could feel their eyes on me, their silence deafening to my fears. "What does that mean?"

"It means you were created for war, Essallie. You're the perfect soldier."

TEN
A LIFE OF LIES

The next few days withered by in an uneven haze. I went through the motions like any other person, only inside I felt trapped. The words *'prisons of fire and destruction'* sounded inside me with every heartbeat, as if my own blood was agreeing with it. It made me feel sick.

I had barely even realized I was distancing myself from my friends. Abigail was the one who took it most to heart. She continued to make it a point to come over to my house and do something, anything, just to see if she could snap me out of my frozen mind. Each day ended virtually the same; her heading off to her car while I watched from the window, emotionless. It was like I had been drained of every emotion in my heart.

Sitting down in the cafeteria, I couldn't help but feel like things were spinning out of control. Each second felt like a blessing and a curse in the same breath, and here I was choking on it. Had it been anyone else they would have relished in the thought of being able to wield fire like some freak-show person you see in the movies. I didn't want any of it.

"...Essallie, did you hear me?" Abigail's voice buzzed into my thoughts, cutting off the notions of how long it would take to down myself. Maybe with fire retarded gloves Kayden could even help.

Looking up from my tray of untouched food I shook my head. "Sorry, lost in thought." I absentmindedly picked up a fork and started to play with the pile of mashed potatoes on my plate.

"I was asking Thomas about that movie we've been wanting to see, Witch in White. Remember the trailer?" She paused long enough to roll her eyes. "Oh wait, of course you don't remember. You've been too busy moping in your corner for freaking ever."

"Easy, Abigail," Thomas muttered.

I set my fork down delicately, locking eyes with Abigail in what I hoped was a perfect death stare. "No, Thomas. She has something to say, let her say it. What's the matter, Abby? Am I not fun enough for you anymore?"

"Not when you're whining like a wannabe emo and shutting yourself in at home every day after school," she snapped. Her lip curled into the tiniest sneer. For a split second I could see exactly why everyone in the school found her annoying. "It never ends with you. You're just like all those other drama queens frolicking around this school sucking up the air."

"Good to know my problems are just a waste of your precious air," I hissed. The burning sensation in my palms began to streak up my arms. I could practically taste the fire begging to be freed from my skin.

"What is wrong with you, Essie?" Her tone dropped to a calmer sound. "You shut me out so fast. Aren't friends supposed to help each other out with their problems?"

I stood up from the chair with a rough shove at the table, my bag swung over my shoulder in the same movement. "Maybe that's just it, Abigail. Maybe you're not so much of a friend to me as I thought you were." I launched past her and out of the room, weaving through the thinned crowd in the hallways toward my car. As soon as I was sure I was alone I yanked up my sleeves. The sharp pinpricks of winter air made my skin practically steam, crackles of blue sparks dancing off of my skin in short bursts. Another minute and I probably couldn't have controlled the fire to protect Abigail or anyone in that room. I climbed into my car and made sure to drive safe home, taking deep breaths to reign in my anger.

Dinner that night was quiet. I still hadn't quite found my appetite.

Jayson seemed to have caught onto my mood. "You normally love chicken alfredo," he pointed out over a mouthful of something fishy. "Did I overcook it?"

"No no, it's fine." I shook my head, eyes glued to the plate. We were eating on the ceramic plates we'd both made as kids. Flowers of all colors and sizes decorated mine. "I'm just sort of thinking of when we were younger. Back when Mom was still around."

I heard him scoff and looked up just in time to see him raise his eyebrows in shock at me. "Why would you want to think of that? Don't you remember what she did to you?"

My eyes drifted back down to my plate. How could I not forget running around the house all night long, hiding in the smallest spaces just to avoid her finding me? Sounds of her thundering footsteps and shrill screeching echoed in my ears. "Can't blame me for wondering if sometimes she was right."

Jayson reached out a hand to place over top mine. His expression was one of pity. "Don't ever think that, Essallie. She was bat-shit and everyone knew it. They say it started long before you came around."

I swallowed a piece of pasta and ignored the churning in my stomach. "What do you mean?" He looked away from me, his expression guarded. "You know more than you're letting on."

He refused to meet my face. Pushing his plate away he blew out his cheeks. "I heard Gram say something once, about how-" he started slow, like each word killed him to speak it, then cut off with no warning. Shaking his head, he rose from the table and took his plate to the sink, the sound of running water hitting porcelain as he scrapped off leftovers. "Mom wasn't exactly a liar. You were a little weird growing up."

Oh, well that was good to know. I heard my voice crack as the words ran over like a broken record in my head. "Weird like she said? A devil's spawn, right?"

The water shut off and Jayson came up behind my chair to place a hand on each shoulder. "No! No, Essie, not like that. You just had a lot of imaginary friends as a kid." He laughed in my ear. "You used to call them your angels. I think that's what freaked Mom out the most."

My mind replayed the night I broke out in my wild fever and the break that came afterwards. Jayson had said I even swore I saw our father. I inched out from the chair and swung around him to dump my plate into the trash. "Thank you for dinner but I'm not really hungry." I didn't wait for him to come up with any reason to save the food; I had the sinking feeling it wouldn't be long before I stopped eating altogether. "Thanks for telling me about my past."

Jayson came to stand in front of the doorway, blocking me in. He waited until I was looking up at him before he spoke. "Our past. Even though we weren't before, we're in this together now."

"Why did you stay here?" I blurted out and instantly regretted it. One heartbreaking truth was more than enough for the day, I wasn't sure if I'd be ready for another. "I always wondered why you never came with me to New York."

He looked oddly confused, as if I had asked him if we lived in Switzerland. "They never told you?" When I shook my head, he frowned. "Gram had said it'd be better if we grew up apart. That we'd do better meeting later when you'd be ready."

I felt the air deflate from my lungs as I tried to picture Gram telling her first grandchild to stay away, like he was poison. Or maybe it was me. Maybe I was the poison she had been trying to protect him from. Had they known all along that I wasn't human? That blood like fire that I could never control ran rampant in my veins? Forcing myself to breathe, I asked the only question burning on my tongue. "Ready for what?"

"I don't know Essallie. I don't know."

————

Saturday came with the perfect break in the weather that I needed. The sky opened up like the heavens spreading their arms wide, the glowing sun offered as the perfect antidote to the constant barrage of snow that had covered everything in town.

I had made sure that I appeared as perfectly normal as I could to Jayson in the morning as he busied himself around the kitchen table before work.

"Could you stop shaking your leg so much? It's kind of creeping me out," Jayson said out of nowhere as he stood in the hallway. His Eskimo suit made him look like an over-puffed marshmallow.

Shoot. I quickly relaxed my leg and shifted my anxiety to tapping my fingers on my arm instead. "So you guys are going to be trying to clear as much of the town as possible?" Apparently some freak storm had hit in the middle of the night, leaving a freshly polished war zone of pure white outside.

"That's the goal. I'd stay home for the day if I were you. That tiny little thing you call a car isn't exactly built for this kind of weather." He turned around and looked like he was going to have a heart attack. "Jesus, Essie, what the hell happened to your face?"

"What?" I picked up the untouched spoon for my cereal to see what he was gawking it. A large purplish bruise crested over my cheek bone and trailed all the way down to my jaw. Surprisingly, it didn't hurt. "Oh, hit the door frame last night going to bed, no worries. And you leave my car alone, Shelly does just fine!" I pouted but quickly hitched a grin to get him to smile. "I don't think I'm going anywhere. But I am going to call the local book store and see if they have the one paperback I need for English."

He nodded while he wrapped his scarf around his neck several times. "Sounds good. I've got a fire going in the living room, don't touch it. It should last until I get back home late this afternoon. And stay away from door frames, sheesh."

"Yes, Mr. Drill-Sergeant. Bye Mr. Drill-Sergeant," I waved him out of the door, doing my best to ignore the glaring white outside. I had a plan on how to take care of that faster than any shovel or snow plow could ever accomplish.

Double-checking the door was shut and Jayson was gone, I sprinted up the steps, rounding the corner and stopping at the first door on the landing. The dark mahogany wood held ornate crested swirls like all of the other doors on the landing, only this one held a subtle shimmer to it, as if someone had meticulously inserted little gems into the wood. Wrapping my hand around the brass knob I twisted it gently to push open the door.

Everything had been covered twelve years ago, back when Mom had been taken to the sanitarium in Portland to *get better* as Gram had told me. Thick cream sheets draped over the canopy bed, but I could still see a peek of the crimson quilted comforter she would wash every morning to have it clean before bed. The brass vanity in the corner probably still held bottles of perfume far past their dates. Even the bookcase had been covered to protect each volume she had bound in some of the most expensive leather she could afford pre-children.

I walked over to her closet and opened the shutters, spotting collections of boxes upon boxes of shoes, photos, her personal journals and more. I kept my eyes peeled until I spotted it in the far top right, just a hairsbreadth away. It was a small ornate music box filled with everything she had for me. I gave a short little leap and latched onto the box, falling to the ground with it pressed tightly to my chest. Mission completed.

Sitting down on the spotless white rug beside her bed I ran my fingers over the lid of my prize. Jewels of varying sizes decorated the top of the box and created a shimmering effect under the thin bars of sunlight that arched through the curtains. Inside was the same stuff from the last time I'd seen it- a birth certificate, two small newborn socks, and one letter folded in half. Taking the parchment from the box and tucking it safely in my pocket, I had all I needed for my trip to see Mommy-dearest for the first time in twelve years.

I took one step through the back door to the house and stopped dead. Snow stood as high as my hips, maybe even higher. Typically I'd turn around and lock myself inside until it turned to July but first there was something I had to see for myself.

Flexing my fingers experimentally I relaxed and let the fire course through my veins, rushing to my fingertips in seconds. Pointing directly at the snow I watched a single jet of fire slice right through it, steam rising.

Excellent.

Hovering my palms just over the snow I let the fire race off of my skin and melt a perfect path straight to my car. Then for good measure I cleaned up the rest of the driveway. Driving down and turning onto the highway I kept the folded piece of paper tightly pressed against my chest.

The two hour drive led me into Portland, the biggest city within several hours. While it wasn't any New York City, it still had everything I could expect it to have, like Starbucks and malls and cramped apartments. I gazed at them pensively, replaying the night of Chase's betrayal and death with a hollow feeling in my chest.

Portland's sanitarium looked nothing like the kind I had seen in movies over the years. A lush and neatly kept landscape rolled around the small property, the building made of brick instead of pure white walling. I followed the signs and parked in one of their small side lots to go inside.

Inside it smelled like someone had washed the walls head to toe in sanitizer. Definitely how I had imagined it. The main white hallway past the reception desk seemed to stretch on forever, doors on either side opening in curiosity to see the stranger walking in their territory.

I took a seat towards the window in the visiting hall. Small tables held scattered checkers and chess pieces and even a few potted plants sat on the windowsills, desperate for sunlight. The far wall with no windows held a collage of paintings done by the patients, all in watercolors. I had started to stand up and see if I could pick out which one my mother could have done when the doors across from me opened and a figure shuffled inside.

At first glance she looked nothing like the mother who used to spend her nights searching the house, desperate to beat the devil out of her own child. She looked frail and brittle, her skin stretched thin over her jutting bones. Deep circles creased under her eyes and blemishes rippled across her skin. But her eyes still held the same crisp stare to them as they had all those years ago.

"You won't find anything of mine on their walls," she spoke in clipped tones and glanced over at the wall. "They find mine too *vulgar*. Might upset the other loonies, you see."

"Good to see you too Mother," I sighed and took my seat again. She sat two seats away, arms crossed reflexively across her chest. Almost every picture of my childhood she had her arms in that pose, but then I never understood why.

She gave me a once-over, her eyes narrowing to slits. "Good to see the demon has still kept you alive. Then again, I doubt you'd do him much good dead."

"No demon is keeping me alive," I bit my cheek to keep my tone reigned in. The heat in my arms raced up and down, ready for any sign of uncontrollable emotion. "Or maybe there is, I don't know. But you're going to explain this to me first." I pulled the letter from my coat pocket and pushed it down the table.

Her eyes locked onto the paper like it was a bug ready to be squished. "You went into my personal belongings?"

"Don't play vulnerable now, Mother. It doesn't suit you," I snapped. "I want you to read that and tell me just who the hell is Michael."

She lifted her head to stare at me with a gaze strong enough to pierce through my heart. "Michael," she breathed. "Is a worthless, ungrateful, disgusting boil of a man." A shaking breath escaped her lips as I watched the stare melt into sorrow. Her bony arms wrapped around her frame as tight as they would go as she fought to keep herself together. "And I loved him dearly."

"Jayson said our father's name was Harry."

"Harry." Now it was her turn to sigh. "Harry was a loyal man and he loved his son very much. But he never loved you. You're the permanent proof that I fell in love with a fool who left me once his task was complete."

I shook my head and tried to add two and two together. "I don't understand. So Michael is my father but he left you knowing you had a baby on the way?"

"Your father," she said with a hysterical laugh. "Let me tell you about your father. Imagine you're in the middle of a crisis and no one can help you. No one but this beautiful man who just happens to lure you home and tell you that together we could have an eternity of love and happiness. That was Michael.

"He said he was here for a mission, which I chalked up to the local church, silly me. I should have put it all together when a month passed and he still hadn't left. But I didn't want to think of that. For the first time in almost two years a man had told me he loved me, that he had wanted me. You wouldn't know what that's like, to have your husband not want to touch you but some handsome mystery man who will.

"After two months of never-ending passion I found out I was pregnant. I knew right from the beginning it wasn't Harry's. So I told Michael, thinking it would promote him to ask my hand, take Jayson and I and make a perfect family. Instead he sat me down, promised me to always love the child inside of me, and left."

I sat there, stunned. What did you say to something like that? What could you say knowing that you were the product of a failed marriage, a broken home? I tried to swallow and found my throat raw and dry like I'd screamed for hours on end.

"Come on," I heard her say, my head immediately snapping up to see her spiteful stare back in place as if she were willing me to wither away. "Did you really think anything different before you came here with that paper?"

My head shook mechanically. "I didn't... not like this. He

left you, Mom, who does that?"

"An angel creating his army." She said it so simply, the roll
of her shoulders practically sending me into a violent rage.
"He said one day he'd be back for you, back for us. I first
thought it meant after your birth. But time passed and before
I knew, it five years had come and gone and still my loving
angel never came back. The only good that ever came from
your birth was that you were an afternoon baby. That, and I
never lost sleep over your birth like I had with Jayson.
Everything else has only been of loss and heartache and
betrayal of your father."

"Good to know I was such a burden. Did he say anything
else?" I pressed past her childish jibes.

She started to shake her head but stopped. "Oh, yes, he
did." Her hands reached up around her neck and fumbled for
something just under her turtleneck. A long silver chain with
a delicate wire wrapped white glass heart was pushed across
the table towards me. Her lips curled into a catty sneer as she
spoke. "He said when you'd see me to give this to you. It was
the only thing your father left me that was pure."

I nodded a numb thanks to her and rose from my seat,
clutching the pendant in my hand. Without looking up I said,
"Guess you were right after all. I guess I really am monster."
She stayed silent as I brushed past her and left but it wasn't
until I was somewhere on the highway that I couldn't shake
off the feeling that she had been staring at me with a malicious
gleefulness. Maybe she was finally happy to know I had
accepted my own fate.

ELEVEN
TASKED WITH ASCENSION

"You're not putting in enough effort. Come on, Essallie, you can do better than this."

I stood in front of Kayden, panting as if I had run the longest marathon of my life at full speed. Not even two days had passed since I had ventured out to see my Mother that Kayden had started harping on me about controlling my abilities. We stood outside in my backyard amidst snow-soaked branches, the barren clay earth beneath my feet a welcoming reminder that life wasn't always filled with the frozen white stuff.

"So what? I don't need to prove anything to you," I wheezed out between gasps for air. My lungs burned as a sharp acidic taste lapped against the back of my throat. Rolling down onto the ground I winced and yanked up my sleeves to see fresh new bruises forming just as the old ones were starting to die off. Kayden had said it was because I wasn't using my gift more effectively, or as he put it, 'on a constant basis.' I told him some days I just didn't feel like setting things on fire and wondering if I was going to accidentally reduce my brother to ashes.

I saw his faint shadow on the ground shake it's head while he muttered something low in a language I didn't understand. "I'm trying to help you and this is the thanks I get? Someone's not getting their World's Favorite Nephilim coffee cup this year."

"You wouldn't know help if it bit you in the-" I stopped and let out a frustrated sigh. "Nevermind. I'm not in the mood for your games today, Kayden."

He stood a few feet away, running his hand through his hair with a bored expression. "Ah, yes, because preparing for the eventual is a game. Silly me. Let's try a new game. How about Monopoly?"

I kicked at the dirt and walked past him towards the house. "Screw your Monopoly."

"What's the matter? Didn't have a good time with Mommy the other day?"

I knew it was a ruse specifically meant to set me off. I shouldn't have reacted, but something within me snapped and ripped at the seams to welcome every venomous thought front and center. A raw scream escaped my throat before I realized it, red coloring everything before me. Something inside of me whispered in a wild tone and I responded without thought, my arms snaking out to release two streams of fire that wrapped around Kayden and sealed him in a constricting grasp. Closing my hands into fists the bands wrapped tighter, his clothes and skin burning wherever the fire touched.

Hands locked I brought them to a cross over my chest, the bands of flame carrying Kayden's dragging frame to stand in front of me. "Who are you," I spat out, "to say anything to me? You only want me to figure this out so you can kill me and move on in your existence as a slimy little leech roaming the plains."

Kayden didn't struggle against the fire; if anything he was grinning, enjoying my display of unbridled power. "You don't understand, you haven't been around as long as I have." A new coil of fire wrapped across his cheek and began to scorch the flesh. "You're a creature created for war. What do you think is going to happen?"

"Nothing is going to h-"

"I'll tell you what's going to happen. Someone is going to find out what you are and use you like the weapon you are meant to be. They're going to drop you in the middle of a war zone and expect you to clear it without hesitation. Are you prepared to defend yourself against the masses of demonic creatures intent on killing you to save their own skin?"

With a shove I released him from his prison, the fire pushing him back halfway across the backyard. He collapsed onto the ground gasping for air, the picture reminding me of a fish out of water. "Don't you ever bring my Mother into this ever again. Understand?"

He stood up and examined the cluster of burns and lacerations covering his body. "Now that's the kind of power I was talking about," he said while prodding at a deep cut on his forearm. Slowly he let his arm dissolve into nothing and reappear intact and unharmed, flexing his fingers for good measure. "Was that so hard?"

"You're impossible," I muttered and turned back and went inside before I decided to let loose on Kayden again. Only next time, I'd probably do more than leave him with a couple of cuts and burns.

The next morning I sat in English hunched over my desk, scribbling violently on a paper. I was starting to feel the drain of my inconsistent emotional state. Food had lost its appeal and sleep was something only the dead were capable of achieving.

A polite cough sounded behind me. "That was a pretty

picture, you know."

I turned up and looked to my side. Leo sat on the edge of my desk with his arms light folded across his chest. Small strands of his thick blonde hair hid most of his brilliant blue eyes. He looked past me to the paper strewn across my desk, one of my eye drawings staring unseeing up at both of us. Small scribbles criss-crossed over half of the eye, making it look like the eye was turning black with disease, violence, or murderous death.

My shoulders rose and fell and I went back to making more scribbles across the details of the iris. "Yeah, I thought it was a good picture at one point too. Too bad we're all disillusioned."

His hand reached out gently to take the pencil from my hand. "There's no illusion in your art, only exposed truth." With a swift move he snapped the pencil in half over his knee and placed both broken pieces on top of my picture. "You look upset. Everything okay?"

I bit back the sigh I ached to let out, to spill every single detail of my unforgiving nightmare that I was nothing more than a blessed dragon in human skin. Since the night of the bonfire Leo seemed to be everywhere I didn't want him to be. We ran into each other in the halls, classes, were assigned as project partners, anywhere I looked he'd be nearby. As if some kind of gravitational pull kept him in my personal orbit, teasing me with things I couldn't have. It could have been doable if Ursula wasn't constantly glued to his hip, shooting daggers at me at any given chance.

I stole a quick glance around the room. No sight of her overly blonde hair. "Shouldn't you be with your precious, porcelain doll?"

His jaw set for a moment before he rolled his shoulders and let out a small breath. "It's nice to get away from the things that suffocate you sometimes. But you still haven't answered my question."

I gave him a bitter smile. "If I told you what was wrong you'd call me crazy."

"Normalcy is overrated." He learned further onto my desk, closing the distance between us until he was hovering above me. "You'd be surprised by how many people hide secrets in this place."

My stomach gave a little roll as I tried to figure out just what he meant by hiding secrets. Heat came off of his skin in waves, begging me to come closer. An image of my fingers running along the skin of his palms, his arms, and up to his neck confused me. Where the hell was this all coming from?

"I...I..." My words caught in my throat. I tried to form the sentence I had planned on saying in my head when a sharp, hot light protruded from my chest. Leo and I immediately looked down, and just under my navy hoodie I felt the heart pendant my Mother had given me *move*. I wrapped a hand around it and stared up at Leo in horror. "Did you see-?"

The door to the classroom opened and our disgruntled teacher stomped inside with an armful of jackets and scarves. "Seats, students! Seats!"

Leo turned back to me for a quick moment. "I'll see you later."

I nodded and prepared to sit through class with a tight knot in my gut. What did Leo think he saw? What if he coughed it up to magic? Wasn't there some sort of law forbidding supernaturals from displaying magic to humans? There had to be, there always was in books and movies. It was practically the golden freaking rule.

Yep, I'm screwed.

The second the bell rang I was over at Leo's desk, my books crammed uncomfortably in my arms. I had to make sure to talk him out of whatever he saw, just in case.

He glanced up and grinned in amusement. "Eager to

continue where we left off, eh?"

"Something like that."

"Good. Follow me." He shuffled his books into a leather messenger bag and slipped it onto his shoulder. We walked out into the hallway and breezed past the lockers and office and headed straight for the parking lot. "Do you trust me?"

I stopped following him and looked up in confusion. "Should I trust you?"

A small sad laugh escaped his lips. "Probably not, but I'm the only one who can tell you about what you are. There's more to Nephilim than that terrible book Ursula has in her *collection,*" he said the word with repulsion.

"Wait, so you know?"

He nodded.

"And you didn't tell me? I just spent the past 40 minutes back there thinking I was going to have to decapitate you or something to keep you quiet about this." I held up the necklace from under my hoodie.

"A trinket from your Maker, no doubt," Leo said and came over to inspect the pendant. "I saw it light up but I can't tell you why. Sometimes it's a demon ward, other times it's for finding your soul mate."

But it didn't glow around Kayden, that much I was sure of. I shook my head to clear the thoughts and re-focus on the main topic. "What do you know about me?"

His eyes danced with mischief and glee, a smirk spreading across his face. "Maybe everything. Maybe nothing at all. You'll have to come with me if you want to find out."

"Fine." I was resolved. I had to know more about what I was, even if it did mean driving off with a guy I barely knew claiming to know more. Besides, I could always just set the car on fire let him burn to a crisp if he tried anything funny. Buckled into our seats I snuck a glance at him out of the corner of my eyes. "Care to tell me where we're going?"

"Nope. But I'll tell you one thing. Where we're going," he reversed the car and pulled out of the parking lot. "That collection of Ursula's is a mere prick of blood compared to the ones you'll soon see."

TWELVE
BETWEEN TWO WORLDS

"Essallie, wake up."

I jolted awake in my seat and flung my hands out in front of me automatically, the rush of heat in my veins lighting fire on my hands. We were still inside of the car, parked outside of a little indie bookstore in what appeared to be some small town in the middle of nowhere.

A silhouette moved next to me. Leo's voice spoke in low tones in my ear. "Please don't light up my parent's car. They haven't finished paying it off yet."

Oh, right. My mind replayed the last few hours over to bring me to speed. Leo knowing I was half-human, the glowing pendant around my neck, the car ride to a place with tons of books. Slowly the fire dulled to a dim flicker on my fingertips before extinguishing itself.

I looked up to see the small neon sign hanging above the tiny shop in front of us. "You're kidding, right? This place is smaller than my bedroom."

Leo bit his lip to stiffen a laugh. He looked half crossed to say something, but stopped and pursed his lips. "You'd think a girl like yourself, the living proof of magic, would put two and two together."

I opened my mouth to retort but he stepped out of the car and motioned for me to follow him. Heat blazed through the door as we stepped inside, and I quickly understood why it was so hot. The shop was cramped and opaque to the point where even light bulbs made little difference in illuminating anything. Every potential walking spot was crammed with clusters of books of all shapes and sizes, the dust thick enough to form thick coating over the skin like gloves.

Twisting through narrow passageways I did my best to avoid stepping on anything. "Who the hell owns this place?"

"My family," he answered without looking back. I followed him around a tightly wound corner. "It's been here since the '30s but no one's actually ran the place since the 70's. We put up wards to keep the occasional human from stumbling upon it and calling the township to demolish it."

Wards? I thought back to one of my favorite fantasy movies where witches casted wards to keep people away from their secret altar. Which meant if they had wards they were protecting something, too. "Is there another book in here on my kind?"

"A book on Nephilim in here? I'd sure as hell hope not. That'd be one heck of a way to ruin something crafted in sacrificed blood." He stopped in front of a shelf in what looked like the furthest corner of the building.

"That book I read was done in blood?" I felt a little nauseous just from recalling it.

"All books on Nephilim are. It's to seal in the history so no one can alter it later or erase it from history. You can't destroy one of those books once it's been properly sealed. Anyone who tries dies." He pushed against the shelf uselessly. "Can't remember how to open it. Shoot."

I stared past him at the shelf and spotted one book that looked freshly cleaned of dust. "That one. Pull it." I said, pointing at the small blue novel. "That's how they do it in the movies. Secret bookcase 101."

Leo stared at me, eyebrows arched high into his hair. He gave the book a light push and the shelf shuddered, swinging inside to reveal a blaze of white light bright enough to reveal the whole room. "Anyone ever told you that too much television is bad and inaccurate?" He ushered me inside and the bookcase softly clicked shut behind us.

It was as if the world had done a 180 around us, swapping everything that was once grimy and old for polished and new. Bookshelves of freshly bound leather and fabric stood neat rows, the floors clean and polished to perfection. White marble pillars connected to high golden arches rested between each bookshelf and held the stained glass ceiling in place.

I couldn't help it; I stared slack-jawed in awe at the pristine perfection around me. Turning to see Leo's impressed grin I felt a light bulb dim to life in my head. "Let me guess. This is also your family's, isn't it?"

"Naturally," he replied with a wink. He walked down the hallway with ease, breezing past other people with a small nod here and a polite smile there while I struggled to keep up with all the twists and turns. "Impressed?"

"Hardly," I lied as we made another turn and came to a stop in what looked like a grand foyer of some sort. Black marble lined the floor, six white marbled pillars bigger than the others holding up an ornately balcony crafted from cast iron and jewels of various sizes and shapes. It instantly reminded me of the box from my Mother's closet.

"Leo, what is this place?" I craned my neck as far as I could to see the delicate pictures that laid out on the ceiling. It showed broad-winged angels floating over gusts of air to a city made of tall towers and sparkling gold. Only the bottom half of the ceiling was shrouded in black, a demon etched into the far corner with horns protruding from his malevolent smile. It looked like a place crafted in the limbo of the world, caught between the darkness of Earth and the precious promise of Heaven.

"Charon," he said. "Home to mythical, the unreal. Your real home."

The second he said it, it instantly felt true. While the house I grew up in felt natural, it never felt real, not like this. This felt natural. A warm that had nothing to do with my powers spread through my body. I was *home*.

I walked in front of Leo and grabbed him by the shoulders. "I want to see it. I want to see it all." Then as an afterthought. "Please."

He laughed and nodded in the same movement. "Where would you like to start?"

"Anywhere. Bookshops, bakeries, anything."

He seemed to think about it for a moment. "I think I know where we should start." His gaze almost looked sad, as if what he was going to say would disappoint me. "There's a tavern just down the main road-"

"Okay," I said. A congratulatory sloshing? "I'm down for drinking until the room tap dances."

"-which is right next to an apothecary. The Alchemist who owns it is married to a lovely woman who knows every history of every kind of person to walk through here," he ignored my interruption and finished. He scratched his head absentmindedly. "They'll probably know where to start looking for anything, considering you're probably the only Nephilim in the past three-hundred years."

"Oh." Guess we'd have to save the sloshing for another kind of celebration. I gave a curt nod. "Lead the way, captain."

He turned and started to walk forward only to stop and spin around rapidly. Any space between us rapidly evaporated, right along with my breath. "Aren't you glad you trusted me?"

"Absolutely," I blurted out without shame. A smile spread across my cheeks faster than I could have imagined possible. It felt like every fiber of my being was singing in joy, the promise of understanding just what I was and where I belonged.

Leo extended his arm to me with a little mock-polite bow. I took his hand and, realizing I was probably breaking some cardinal rule about holding hands with other people's boyfriends, dropped it.

"No, it's okay," he said with a smile but the shock of his words read in his eyes. Every mental alarm in my head sounded off that it was a bad idea. These new surroundings were really starting to scramble my brain with what was right and wrong. This time he reached out and took my hand, holding it firmly in his grasp as I did my best not to blush or read into it.

We took our time walking down the street, Leo stopping to let me stare in a shell-shocked awe of everything around me. The city looked exactly as it had on the glass ceiling; towers of white spiraled into the clouds farther than the eye could see. Smaller brick-and-mortar houses were crafted of the same blemished white marble I had seen inside of the library, coils of golden-twisted metal lacing along the outer frame like imitation vines. Paved tawny colored cobblestones led down a wide expanse of road that ended in a cul-de-sac lined with several small shops.

It felt weird staring at everything but it was something I wanted to record to memory in case I never saw it again. Witches and wizards, goblins and centaurs, faeries and more walked past us at any given moment, each one different from the first and the last. I half expected to pinch myself and wake up from a daydream in school.

"What are you doing?" Leo asked as he watched me pinch myself for the third and fourth time.

"Trying to see if I'm going to wake up," I answered truthfully. "This just feels so..."

"Impossible? Imaginary?"

"Yes."

"Well, is the fire you create impossible? Is that imaginary?"

"Impossible, yes," I said with a laugh. "Scientifically speaking, anyway. Imaginary?" I thought back to the first night I felt the heat in my fingers, how I had thought I'd burnt them on the bonfire. How fast everything had changed from there. "No."

Leo smiled at me and gave my shoulder a nudge with his own. "Let's head inside. His wife is going to love seeing you."

Inside the shop it was darker, a thin cloud of smoke hovering against the ceiling. The upper half of all four walls held shelves sporting different bottles of color, shape, and size while the lower half had tables spread every few feet draped in ornate fabric and scrolls of parchment. At the back nestled between two tables stood a desk just as elegant as everything else, an old man twirling the ends of his white mustache while he gazed into a mirror standing behind it.

"Excuse me," I started off.

"Shh shh shh shh *shhhhhhhh*." The old man held up a finger in protest, eyes never leaving the mirror. His fingers drifted from the mustache to his bald scalp to the tips of his sharply pointed ears. "The sign outside said I was out to lunch. You'll have to come back later."

"We're not here for a remedy," Leo spoke beside me. "We're here to see your wife, Lorena."

The man pulled his face away from the mirror and I let out a little gasp. Bronze colored scales covered the center of his face from the top of his eyebrows just under the chin. Cat-like eyes with violet irises blinked back at us as he regarded us with curiosity.

"My Lorena? Heavens, what did the woman do now?" He

rolled his eyes and gave a haughty little sigh. "LORENA! SOME KIDS ARE HERE TO SEE YOU!"

Curtains behind the desk parted as a small, brittle looking woman gently inched out, a curious expression drawn on her face. Lines of both laughter and worry creased into her skin and time hovering over potions had hunched her shoulders into a permanent hump. But her eyes still shined like two commanding orbs of opal that could rip the truth right out of your lips.

"Kids? I don't recall anyone making an appointment." She smacked the back of the man's head as a bell rang behind us. "Next time lock the door."

I shifted uncomfortably in my shoes, exchanging a pleading look with Leo. I wasn't ready to show them my power, not with Kayden's warning still swirling around my head.

"Lorena, we came to see you on the word of my father, Artemis? We own the library just down the street," Leo spoke in a silky-smooth tone, making sure to inch closer to her. I watched him bat his eyelashes, one tiny step away from pleading on his hands and knees. "Remember?"

"Cut the flirtatious crap," Lorena cut him off. She shooed at him as if he were no more than a stray that had snuck in off the streets. "Wealthy business boy, that's all you are. Leave us be and play your pranks on someone else."

"But this isn't a-"

A hand shoved right into his face and cut him off. "*Leave.* Before I find that useless father of yours and give him a good crack on the skull." Her tiny frame inched back behind the curtain as she went off on a rant under her breath.

"You heard the lady," the old man chimed in as he shrugged with a bored expression glazing over his eyes. "Now could you leave? I really don't want to sleep on the couch tonight and the longer you stay the more likely that's going to happen."

Leo and I turned to look at each other. I could feel the defeat in his saddened resolve of a stare, his lips clenched tight in a bitterly depressive smile. To come so close only to be shuffled aside by the very woman holding the secrets I needed...fire blazed over my knuckles.

Jingle bells sounded again from the doorway, the same time someone cleared their throat. I looked over to see a willowy shaped figure hiding under a maroon cloak beckoning us closer. Crimson fingernails longer than her actual fingers reached out from the cloak, the skin on the hand a sickly lime green.

"Follow me, *Nephilim*, and bring your little friend too." A girlish chipper voice sounded from under the hood before turning around and abruptly leaving the shop.

The fire vanished from my knuckles and I grabbed Leo's hand, yanking him back out onto the street before the door could shut behind the cloaked woman. Crowds of people pushed up and down the street to the point where I could barely make out anyone. The tip of a maroon hood caught my eye as it entered a pub halfway up the street. I instantly sprinted down the way, praying Leo wouldn't trip and take us both down in one fell swoop.

While the outside of the pub looked regal and designed for a couture world, the inside resembled any regular run-of-the-mill drinking hot spot. A couple unsavory looking creatures sat at the counter, a lizard tale sticking out of the back of one of the guy's pants 'accidentally' getting a little too friendly with a waitress and her short skirt.

Leo inched a little closer to me, his shoulders set in a rigid stance. "I don't like the looks of this place."

I thought back to the bars I'd seen in New York City, memories of vomiting and outside brawls coming back to mind. Judging by how this bar still had its floors polished and no shattered glass to be seen it looked marvelous to me.

I offered him a sweet smile. "It's not bad. Almost has a type of rustic charm to it." A green hand waved at a booth across the room, the hood still hiding her face. "Come on." This person already knew what I was, so it was time to see just how deep the waters were. I let Leo slide into the far end of the booth, his uncomfortable behavior still beyond obvious. Last thing we needed was a brawl against Lizard Tale and his groupies from the counter.

The hooded figure seated across from us giggled. "Good to know you can track a faerie."

"I'd thank your cape for that, not for any skills you think I may have," I said. Arms crossed against my chest I made sure to give my best look of revulsion. "What did you call me before?"

"Do you really want me to say it aloud in here?" The hood leaned closer and pressed both hands onto the table. "Around all these ears?"

Kayden's warning played in my head again. I leaned back in my seat and glared into the hood as Leo shifted closer beside me. "Okay, let's just say what you said earlier was right. What do you know about it?"

"Give me your arm," the hood instructed. Instantly I drew both closer to my chest.

"How about we see who the hell you are for starters," I growled. The heat of my fire swirled in my chest, ready to spread at any given moment I let my guard down. "Or you can keep pushing me and watch this whole place go up in flames."

Leo's horrified expression came into view from the edge of the table. But I caught the faintest touch of a smile grace his lips as his eyes flashed with a hidden delight. "Essallie, you're not serious. You wouldn't."

I cracked my knuckles, watching the sparks jut off in

different directions. Small scorch marks littered the table between us and I did my best attempt at a wicked smile. "Want to bet your life on it?"

"Okay, okay," the hooded figure held out both hands like a white flag. Her long fingernails pulled back the hood in a single graceful move, revealing a beautiful face. Her skin was of the same lime green as her hands save for a large navy blue blemish that covered one of her caramel colored eyes and part of her cheek. Ears nearly twice as long as her head extended back into thin points, most of them hidden in the thick caramel colored curly mass of hair that rested on a shoulder in a half-pony tail. "My name is Serena. Satisfied?"

"Much," I said with little enthusiasm. Part of me wished she had kept the hood on. I suddenly felt very plain compared to her wild appearance. "Tell us what you know."

She stretched out a hand for a second time, fingers moving impatiently. "Give me your arm."

I rolled up my sleeve and held out my arm for her, doing my best to ignore the stares from the bruising that covered nearly every inch of my skin. She seemed unfazed by it and turned over my arm to expose the lighter skin underneath. She began to trace the patterns of my veins, lightly putting pressure on certain spots were the blue showed up stronger.

Her stare was guarded, cautious. "And how long has the bruising been going on?"

"Not too long. Kayden said it had something to do with using my power in bursts instead of all day," I frowned at her. "Why?"

She exchanged a dark glance between Leo and myself. "Everything I am about to tell you is going to make you wish you had never made it past birth."

I felt a shiver run down my spine. I wasn't sure how much more bad news I could take. Against my inner voice telling me to run back home and hide, I nodded. "Please."

Serena released my arm and sat back in her chair, a solemn expression on her face. "Your power has already come into full bloom, that is why you are bruising. Why you feel the heat of anger in here." She pointed at her chest with a long fingernail. "Nephilim are not meant to tap into their full power until they ascend with the proper binding rituals performed between themselves and their Watcher." She inclined her head toward Leo. "You have found your Watcher here, have you not?"

Leo shook his head and laughed nervously. "No, we hardly know each other."

"And you think that matters to the fate that was decided for you centuries ago?" Serena blinked her caramel eyes with mock amusement. "I can see it between the two of you, the bond is strong just under the surface. You will understand your calling soon enough, mortal."

I felt the color drain from my face. "What if he isn't, though? How are you supposed to know or find someone like that?"

"You will find them, as they will find you. A natural pull will bring you together when you do not expect it. A Watcher is connected to their Nephilim by a cosmic birthright- you both will have to have been born on the same day, year, and time." Her fingernails tapped in a lazy rhythm across her cheek as she recited the facts with a dull, dry tone. "If not, then you die."

I shot forward in my seat, leaning across the table to the point where my nose was touching hers. "What do you mean I die?"

"Sit down, child." She gave me a shove back into my seat. "I said die. Those bruises on your flesh? That's the beginning. Without the proper ritual to bind your magic in check your blood will burn while you live. Destroy you from the inside out until nothing is left."

My mind started to swirl like a non-stop carousel ride. It wasn't enough to have uncontrollable powers or to be told that I was to be a weapon of war. Now I had to find someone, my personal protector, to complete a ritual that would save me from burning alive from the inside out by my own blood? I felt sick.

Raising shakily from my seat I took in a small breath. I made sure to keep my hands in my pockets to keep them from shaking in front of Serena and Leo. "I think it's time we leave. Leo, can you take me home?"

He nodded and rose from the booth to stand by my side, a hand on my shoulder. "Thank you, Serena, for the information."

"Don't thank me," she pursed her lime green lips in thought. "I'm only doing what was told of me a long time ago." She turned and looked at me. "Don't look at it as a death sentence, deary. Look at it as a new outlook on life. I know I sure would."

THIRTEEN
INVITING DEATH WITH GRACE

The next day at school dragged like no other. After returning home from Charon, my little magical wonderland, I wasn't able to sleep. My room had felt foreign, like someone had re-arrainged the furniture or had gone through my things. Jayson had sworn twice he didn't do a thing but I knew boys could do something as little as plant a dirty sock in a corner and wait for someone to find it for weeks. That's how I felt. I was the sock in the corner left behind to be found weeks later, reeking to high heavens and possibly on fire.

At lunch I made sure to apologize to Abigail for being the biggest bitch since Marie Antoinette and offered to make it up with a movie. It was a good idea because it would keep my mind off of the rest of the chaos swirling around me. It was good twice over because it kept me from packing the first bag I could and skipping back to Charon to leave everything behind.

I left the cafeteria feeling good, giving Abigail a hug and parting ways as I left for History and her for her Art class. Halfway to my classroom the crowd in the hall thinned, then vanished altogether.

Something swung at me from around the corner and I turned in time to have a textbook connect with the side of my face. I slammed back into the lockers behind me. Ursula stood above me, a textbook clutched in her hands.

"What the *hell* is your problem?" I yelled at her, unsteadily stumbling back to my feet.

She swung at me again, blonde hair covering half of her face. "*You're my problem!*" I stepped to the side to avoid her third swing and knocked the book out of her hands. "What did you do to Leo?"

"What do you mean what did I do? You're the idiot who won't give him any breathing room!" I screamed back at her. My fists clenched in case I needed to give her a little reality check.

She let out a wild scream and lunged for me, manicured nails sharpened to little claws. "Liar! Someone saw you holding hands in Charon. You can't hide from me, Essallie Hanley." She spat on my shoes.

"Oh hey, look at that. You're a real lady after all," I taunted with little care. I was sick and tired of her teenage-drama problems and constant level of immaturity picking on other people for no reason. And I knew just where to wound her, hard.

Backing a little further away from her grasp I began. "I bet Leo liked it when I kissed him. He probably thought it was nice to kiss something that hasn't been around sucking face with every male she's met since birth!"

"You're a terrible liar. They would have told me if you had kissed him. I wouldn't have let you live through the night if you had." She took a step closer as I took a step back. "Did he show you the apothecary in Charon? How about the library? His favorite bakery? He probably only showed you the door to your little grimy motel bed."

I let out a sharp crack of a laugh. "No honey, that was you with the married men you slept with, I'm sure." Fire blossomed over my knuckles like a warning of the blaze yet to come. "So I held his hand while I played tourist. Are you really going to try and bash my head in over that?"

Ursula stopped for a second and thought about it. "Yes, yes I am." In a move faster than I had anticipated she snatched the book off the floor and took a sharp swing at my head.

The book flew out of her hands and landed behind her with a dull thud. Ursula stared at me in confusion which quickly turned to a violent rage, raising her hands to try again in scratching at me. Kayden was immediately behind her, hands holding her upper arms in an immobilizing grasp. I watched, frozen in shock, as he drew her against his chest and held her in place while she kicked and screamed.

"Relax, Ursula, relax," he whispered repeatedly in her ear. "She didn't do anything with him, I promise."

"How would you know?" I sneered and Ursula instantly responded by thrashing even harder than before against Kayden's prison hold. "I don't remember inviting you along."

"Someone has to keep an eye on you and I didn't find pretty boy Leo up for the job," he replied casually, shrugging his shoulders with an alien grace. "You really are terribly bad at the whole 'keeping your powers a secret' thing, you know. Truly, terrible."

"So what?" I retorted bitterly. "Now I need a freaking babysitter every time I don't walk out of the house with you?" I pointed a shaking finger to the struggling body in his arms. "You might as well let her murder me then, because that's exactly what you're doing, Kayden. You're keeping me on a leash I can't even see and sooner or later it's going to choke me."

Ursula had stopped struggling in his arms, reduced to a pile of whimpering sobs. Rivulets of mascara ran down her cheeks and she hung her head against the side of one of his arms. "He's all I have, Kayden, he's all I have."

"Oh please," I groaned with a roll of the eyes. "You'll find another human when he dies, I'm sure of it."

"You don't understand!" Her head lifted back up to stare at me, her eyes watery orbs still spilling over her cheeks. "He means everything to me. Imagine living a life where you can't control any desire you've ever had, a life where everything you touch breaks." She took in a shaking breath as her voice warbled to the point of breaking. "A life beyond your control, where you'll do anything to have back a sense of normalcy, a sense of heart. Then you've grasped just a fraction of what I've gone through."

"He's one human on your list, Ursula. How is this one different than all the others you loved and killed?" My head shook as I let out a low laugh. If anyone had ever told me I would be seeing the beauty queen of Belfast stand before me, sobbing no less, I'd of told them to of lay off the drugs.

Her pitiful gaze lingered as she continued to stare, her eyes locked on me. Sensing she wasn't going to attempt murder soon, Kayden slowly released her from his grasp until she stood on her own. "He's not *just some human* to me, he never was. Every day he lives, every day our relationship continues is proof to me that I can break my cycle." She laughed darkly and swiped at the tears beading under her eyes. "Most succubi love it. They love to kill the man or woman they've just slept with, feeding off of their energy, this life-force inside of them. Human blood is a potent drug like no other. I don't want it, I never wanted anything to do with it. Dying would be a gift. You should be grateful you get to die."

For the first time, I saw something human in Ursula, and it certainly wasn't what I had expected. Envy came off of her body in leaps, the effect being the same as if she had been screaming in my face for hours on end. I didn't doubt for a moment that didn't love Leo, love him enough to make sure nothing was going on between us. He was her sanity card, her remaining tie to whatever piece of humanity she had left, and should that tie ever break, it would be her undoing.

Kayden stood off to the opposite side of the hall, leaning against a locker with arms crossed over his chest. He looked as human and Ursula and I did but we all knew it was just a single mask from the many he could pull out on a whim to disguise himself with. I wondered if he still had any ties to humanity, if someone or something could make him weak in the knees and give up everything just to see them smile. As if he heard me our eyes met, his expression one of someone holding a closely guarded secret. The saying 'dead men tell no tales' echoed in my head, but Kayden was very much not-alive and definitely had stories to tell.

"Take a picture, it'll last longer," he said with a sneer, the corners of his mouth hitching into a smile.

"Do demons even show up on film?" I half-asked, matching his smile. "Or do they only exist in the minds of the insane?"

Ursula picked up her textbook from the floor, holding it against her. "Oh, he definitely shows up in film. I have a photo from the '50s in my bedroom." Then her eyes lit up brilliantly. "I have an idea!"

"Quick, look for the smoke," I stage-whispered to Kayden as she started to grin even bigger. "Or fire, just look for a big ball of fire."

Running up to stand directly in front of Kayden she let her smile spread wide enough to almost split her face into two. "The Charon Carnival is this weekend, I say the four of us go. There's got to be a huge chance for her to find her protector-thingy Leo told me about." She turned over to me, the excitement so fierce on her face it was like staring into the blinding sun. "What do you say?"

I looked at Kayden, who seemed completely neutral on the idea, to Ursula, who looked like an eccentrically decorated hot air balloon from her platinum blonde hair to shining blue eyes more dazzling than sapphires. The idea of seeing the rich marble city decorated like a big top circus sounded almost like a potentially favorite dream or a perfectly beautiful nightmare.

"Do I need to wear a costume?"

Both of them grinned.

———

Everything had been planned down for the weekend of the carnival. Ursula made sure to stop by and give Jayson her sweetest smile of innocence, and a little hint of her persuasion as she gushed about how much fun we were going to have at her house over the weekend. Jayson didn't need any further details and it gave me the perfect cover to spend a night in Charon in a home owned by one of Ursula's friends, sporting the perfect balcony to see the fireworks display at midnight.

Kayden, Leo, and Ursula all had costumes from a small shop inside Charon for the occasion. Kayden had offered up several of Ursula's previous outfits for the day, but I politely declined once I saw the bare midriffs and abundance of crimson and canary colored lace. I was still short on an idea and the weekend was approaching- fast.

Standing in front of the mirror in the bathroom two nights before the carnival was to begin I pouted and examined my face. Still the same parchment colored skin, still the same bottomless brown eyes and short blonde hair. Twisting the ends of my hair, my thoughts turned back to that fateful day in the boutique with Cassie. Part of me wondered if the outcome would have been different had I skipped the party like my instincts had told me. Or if I ever would have found out about just how damaged my mother was from my father's actions if I hadn't moved back home.

My fingers traced around the edges of the white heart pendant that hung from my neck. As if in response to my touch it glowed with a sharp pulse of pure light. A light bulb went off in the back of my head and I went for my closet, pushing aside my shirts and jackets to reach a pink bag in the far corner. I unzipped the bag and examined the layers of white organza, satin and peeking hints of lace that made up my mother's wedding dress for the marriage she never had with my father.

It was perfect for a carnival of the inhuman.

FOURTEEN
HEAVY HEART TO CARRY

Standing outside of the little bookshop Friday night, Kayden and I waited for Leo and Ursula to meet up with us. The temperature had dropped dramatically as the sun was far under the horizon, the cold enough for little snowflakes to fall and dissolve just as they touched the ground. In the empty expanse of land around us, it was peaceful and calming.

Kayden let out a long-winded, irritated sigh. "We should have all just rode in the same car. Or I could have flown us all here. Why the need for separate vehicles?"

Normally I would have told him to shut up, but even after an hour with him I was still unable to get over his outfit. He was dressed in a skin-tight suit of rich satin, blood red and virgin white made for a jester of the court, three pointed jingle hat and all. A black star had been painted over each eye to act as his mask.

I opened my mouth to say something only to take one look at him and break out in laughter all over again as I pictured him trying to juggle and failing miserably. "I never knew a jester could look so cute and so handsome all at once."

For a split second it looked like he could have blushed under his dark skin. He seemed to be at a loss for words. "You, uh, look nice too."

I looked down to my feet, my face growing hot. If only he knew the hours of careful make-up and jewelry selecting I had done. For a mask I had taken red lace and draped it over my eyes, cutting out two small holes and making sure to tie it in a neat bow in the back. Against the creamy color of my skin and the white of the dress it contrasted perfectly. I pulled the black floor-length pea coat across the front of my dress and let out a small exhale.

Kayden's feet shifted closer. He had tilted his head down to me, a small smile dashing his painted red lips. "I mean it. It's very fitting. You look, what's the word, regal."

"You're only saying that."

"I'm not," he said quietly. "I'd never lie to you about something like that."

The honesty in his voice brought out a surge of confidence in me I hadn't felt in weeks. I glanced up and down the road for any sign of headlights before I locked eyes with Kayden. "I want you to try something."

He raised an eyebrow in question, then gave me a once-over. "You never really took me for the kinky type, but I never say no."

I punched him in the arm as hard as I could, sparks flying off from the contact. "No, you idiot. Something else. But I'm going to need your help." I bit on my lower lip as I thought of how to say what was on my mind. "I...don't want to hurt you."

"I'm listening."

"I want you to kiss me," I blurted out a little faster than I'd of liked. My face grew hot instantly, and I zeroed my focus on one of the jingle bells ringing on his hat. "To see if I can control the fire inside. That's all."

I had expected to hear him laugh, to mock me or call me crazy. Instead he came close enough until I couldn't get away from his eyes. The color had turned to a molten amber with swirls of the onyx black I'd come to know as his favorite choice. "It's okay if you burn me." He reached up gently and placed a finger under my chin.

The fire was instant, flames spreading over his hand as if he had dunked it in a bucket of gasoline and thrown a lit match onto it. I stumbled back, careful not to dirty the dress on the damp, muddy ground.

"I wasn't ready," I apologized. "Give me a second."

Kayden stepped back, waiting.

Eyes shut, I focused on my breathing, making sure to keep it even. The burning sensation of the fire coiled inside, but it wasn't volatile. I imagined extinguishing most of the flame and pictured cool, refreshing air taking place inside of my chest. Inside I felt lighter, calmer, like I could control it long enough to hold back the flame.

Stepping forward, I came up to him and nodded. "I'm ready."

He moved slow, eyes never leaving mine as he watched for the tiniest change in my heart. His fingers grazed the edge of my chin lightly, and when nothing happened he ran his fingers along my cheek.

Inside my heart was pounding, thundering like a violent wind storm. I leaned in closer and without thinking, pressed my lips against his.

Everything stopped.

A heat different than anything I had ever felt before, different than my personal fire bloomed to life, spreading a comforting warmth to every inch of my body. His breath was freezing where mine was scalding, the mixture creating a sensation like no other to run through my veins and sing for mercy. Hands that weren't mine encompassed my face and held me close to stop me from running away. I flung my arms around his waist and prayed he didn't dissolve into the smoky dust I'd come to know.

In the distance I heard a door slam shut, two excited voices growing closer and closer.

Kayden's lips froze. He pulled back with a sharp jolt, staring at me with a look I couldn't quite place, like he was torn between desire, longing and bitterness all at once. Eyes black as coal, he turned away from me and walked up to the car to lean against the frame. "Guess your experiment worked after all."

I nodded numbly, tasting the lingering sensation on my lips. A cold and hollow sensation settled into my bones, my skin aching for another moment of his hands on my face. This wasn't right; I wasn't supposed to like the man who had tried to attack me, who showed me what kind of a monster I was. Yet here he was, scrambling my brain into silly putty for the molding.

"Kayden, I-" I started to say when Ursula and Leo showed up, each dressed for the show. Ursula had spun her hair into a tight bun of curls piled high, small ringlets hanging down and around her face. Her dress was of a shimmering silver fabric that clung to her every curve, a deep slit riding up to mid-thigh and exposing her thin, willowy legs. She looked as ethereal as an angel should be, something I could never achieve. Leo on the other hand stayed very modest, sporting a standard black and white tuxedo with black shoes, his hair slicked back.

He grinned as soon as he laid eyes on me. "Very classy."

"You look like a god-damn penguin," I replied with a smirk, giving him a shove. Any form of tension that had lingered on my mind before instantly vanished with his smile.

"Excuse me, are we going to go or just stand here in this bitchin' cold and talk about how Leo looks like he's twelve in that suit?" Ursula tapped her foot impatiently. "Leo, your keys."

"Alright, alright woman, I'm going," he muttered but winked at her before opening the door. It was darker inside than out, dust floating out into the nighttime sky as we shuffled in, doing our best to avoid each other's feet and outfits. Past the library passageway connecting Charon to the book shop in Maine and the library itself was where it all really began to unfold.

Outside the grand library it looked like a time warp had taken place. The large cobblestone main street had been decorated lavishly in handcrafted paper lanterns floating in mid-air, adding a subtle glow to the shops that had each been decorated for the event. Bakeries turned into makeshift pie stands, clothing stores now had tailored ringmaster hats and dramatic costumes, and carnival people wandered through the crowd to give small demos of juggling and sword swallowing. Off on the side streets sat rides, from tea cups to mini-roller coasters, even a haunted house and house of mirrors.

Kayden swiped a spool of cotton candy for me as the four of us took our time down the main street, only to come to a halt down at the end. Where the cul-de-sac had been before now stood a big top unlike anything I had ever seen, it's red and white stripes classic. A large arch made of twisted black iron held up a banner showing an image of a big-top, lions and tigers, and clowns.

"Is this what we're seeing?" I asked excitedly, passing off the cotton candy to Leo, who happily devoured the rest. "A circus show?"

"No, we're here to eat Chinese and make out with the bearded lady," Kayden rolled his eyes but was obviously trying hard not to smile. He inclined his head to the masses of people behind us all making their way to the big top with the rest of us. "That's what a circus is for, isn't it?"

"I would sure hope you're here for the show," someone purred beside us. Serena was dressed in a tight corseted black top laced with spider web grey strings and low-rise liquid black pants that revealed an exposed midriff covered in delicate jewels glued to her skin. Her hair had been pulled into a tight bun behind her head and her caramel eyes were surrounded by kohl smudging with rose red painted lips. "You'll get to see me perform the act I've been practicing for months." And with that she vanished behind the curtain of the entrance.

We paid for our tickets and stepped inside. The big-top looked nothing like a traditional circus and yet it looked every bit like a step back to the 1920's. A bustling lobby with a full coat check, concession stand and roomy seating in hand-stained leather chairs led to a set of majestic stairs carpeted in traditional red. Low lighting gave everyone a soft glow to their complexions, making the diamonds and rubies every woman wore glimmer with a tantalizing glow.

I checked my coat in and turned around, praying I blended in. Even though I wasn't the only human in the room I felt my white dress with the extra layers stand out, the bodice corset with a sweetheart neckline suddenly too revealing. I brought along small white gloves to cover my ring less hands and made sure to double check my red laced mask was still in place.

When I turned around to find Kayden for our seats he was nowhere to be found. Leo was reading a small pamphlet on the history of Fae, lost in his own little world.

"Leo, have you seen Ursula or Kayden?" I nervously asked, tugging on the hem of my gloves.

Looking up from his reading he stared around in confusion. "They were here a second ago." He scratched his head while frowning, scanning the crowd until he pointed. His face quickly turned from relief to worry. "There they are, talking to the Queen."

"Judging by your tone I'd say that isn't a good thing."

"Let's just say," Leo quietly muttered, pretending to adjust his bow tie. "Few are on her good side, and even fewer who were on her bad lived long to tell about it." He quickly changed the subject. "Listen, while we have a minute alone, I need to tell you something."

Smiling, I gave him a little shoulder nudge. "Sure. What's up?"

He looked around the room before pulling me aside to a corner of the lobby. "I know we're not supposed to be seeing each other like this, because Ursula thinks we're getting all close and lovey, but I have to explain something to you." He took a deep breath. "I think I might be your Watcher. I've been having these weird visions, like these clips of memory-"

"Leo." I took his hands and gave him a sad smile. "Don't listen to what that woman- what Serena had said. She said we'd have to have matching birthdays right down to the minute."

Still resolved, he leaned closer. "Tell me your birthday."

"March seventeenth," I said with a little irritability. "Please, let's not go down this road. We're here to have fun tonight and-"

"My birth date is March seventeenth," he barely said above a whisper. His hands slipped from my grasp and cupped them instead. "At 4:35 in the afternoon."

I shook my head and started to speak over his increasing protests. "I don't even know what time I was born. Listen, Kayden and Ursula are going to come over here and get the wrong idea."

"What idea would that be?" Ursula snapped from behind me. Her face looked livid, as if someone had lit a roman candle under her behind. She reached out past me and took a hold of Leo's arm, pulling him to her side. "That you're flirting with him yet again? You'd better be damn thankful I don't have anything heavy to swing at you with tonight, Essallie."

"Would you just get the hell off your high horse?" My voice grew as I stepped closer, fists clenched tight. One good shot in the face and she'd never have to worry about any male ever loving her again, least not physically. "He was sharing an idea with me about finding my Watcher. You know, that person I'm supposed to bind to and save my soul from burning alive?"

"Quite frankly," she seethed between her pearly whites. "I don't give a damn if you find your person and live or burn to a crisp like a piece of processed fish stick. Let's go, Leo." She pulled him up the steps and out of sight, my last glimpse of Leo being his pitiful stare as he looked over his shoulder, mouthing something to me.

"Essallie, have a minute?" Kayden came over, his expression neutral. I wondered if I had pissed him off somehow, too. "There's someone I'd like to introduce you to."

A tall, thin dark haired woman with skin as fair as buttermilk came around Kayden, dressed in a long flowing gown of fabric that reminded me of the midnight sky. Her dark brown almond shaped eyes matched the perfect pout of her lips and light blush on the tops of her cheekbones. Black hair spun in a perfectly slick braid coiled like a tamed snake over her shoulder and down to her hips. While her body appeared frail and dainty her presence was one that commanded power without question.

"So you must be the Nephilim, a first in over three hundred years. What a curious race, one foot in the realm of immortals, one in the realm of death," the Queen lamented with a kind smile that didn't touch her eyes. She gave a small nod and turned swiftly to head up the stairs, the train of her dress flowing. "The show's about to start, let us go."

"Come on, let's get to our seats," Kayden took me by the arm and led us into the fabric just past the stairs. We found ourselves at the top of a staggeringly high set of stadium seating. A small space halfway down, two empty chairs, awaited us.

We took our seats just as the lights were dimmed, a single spotlight trained on the center ring of the circus stage down below. Trumpets blaring an intimidating opening fell quiet as drums pounded. A gentleman, the balding man who owned the Apothecary, stepped out to the sound of rigorous applause and whistles. His emerald green suit went against the bright red shoes and checkered print blouse he wore.

"Greetings all to the Circus of Bizarre, an annual tradition here at Charon! I am the great Ringmaster Rooney here to show you everything that will go wrong, silly, and downright mischievous," he finished with a twist of his mustache. "Be patient ladies and gentlemen, for a surprise waits behind our door, like our residential lion full of roar!"

A light came to life in the far left end, spotlighting a woman in a nude suit and a fake crest of hair framing her face. She gave a sultry little pose before morphing into a full-sized lion. The crowd started to clap enthusiastically as I seemed to be the only one confused.

Leaning in to Kayden's shoulder I did my best to whisper as quietly as I could. "They're using shape-shifters instead of real animals?"

He nodded enthusiastically as he kept his eyes glued to the circus floor. "That's our version of a circus. In case you haven't noticed, we don't really follow a standard protocol."

I sat back in my seat, frowning. A circus was supposed to be about animals doing tricks, knowing that at any given moment they could snap and eat the ringmaster or go insane and stampede through the crowd. But who was I to judge? It had been obvious from the start that nothing ran like it did in the mortal half of the world. It was only fitting a circus would be as perversely weird and as unusually different than anything else in the world.

The acts continued one by one, each animal starting off as a beautiful woman dressed in a nude suit with a piece of their animal to decorate with. Lions, tigers, rhinos, even elephants all came to life on the stage, each performing a couple of tricks before returning to the dark shadows of the floor.

After several displays of boa constrictors spelling words in the ground, the ringmaster spoke as loud as he could over the wild applause. "And now, for the grand finale I give you the beautiful Cassandra and her half-demon lover Chase as our entangling trapeze duo!"

I felt my blood turn to a cold sludge and thunder in my ears. Immediately I started shaking Kayden violently and searching for the nearest exit. "We have to leave right now. If Cassie's here that means she's going to see me and her and Chase will kill me and- Kayden?"

Kayden hadn't moved an inch despite everything I had said. His eyes looked permanently frozen in a gleeful stare to the center of the circus stage. One look around confirmed it; hundreds of faces all had the same cheerful smile and doll-eyed wide eyes focused on the floor down below.

"Pity, isn't it? That your little precious boy toy is unable to help you need it most," a catty voice sounded from above. Cassie sat on one of the trapeze swings as it gently rocked back and forth. "I can't imagine what that could be like. Oh, wait."

I stood up from my seat, taking in more frozen faces. "You're supposed to be dead. Kayden killed the two of you that night in the apartment, I saw it!"

"Please." She jumped off the swing and landed soundlessly onto a couple of steps below. "You watched Chase die, we both did. He never killed me."

She looked nothing like the Cassie I had remembered from

our days of sharing secrets in class, of sleepovers and shopping excursions. Her uncut knee-length black hair had been traded in for a short violet bob. Patches of colors randomly appeared on her skin, making her look bruised one minute and colored in with a sharpie the next. This wasn't my Cassie, not any more. The Cassie I knew had long since been swallowed alive and offered like fodder to her inner turmoil to look forever young.

"Must be so proud, being a necromancer and all," I said slowly, calling my inner fire to every inch of my body. Like Kayden, if she touched me she'd be engulfed in flames in a matter of seconds. "How is Chase?"

"Why don't you ask him for yourself? I'm sure he'd love to chat before ripping out your heart like that demon did to him," she hissed but stayed in place. "Are you surprised to see us? Shame we had to catch you off guard like that, but it's really all for Chase over there. You see, he loves the taste of fear in blood."

Taking another step backward I nodded, encouraging her to keep talking. I could feel the sensation of my fire just under the fingertips of my skin, ready for action. "How did you know where to find me? Charon isn't exactly a high-traffic area."

"But it is for supernaturals like yourself," she skittered closer, closing the gap I'd been creating between us. "You needed to find your calling, a little place to call home. Chase said it would only be a matter of time before you showed yourself asking about what you were." She shook her head and laughed. "Such a silly little freak."

The pendant around my neck began to glow in spurts and flash like a warning signal. Cassie looked down for the smallest second, taking her eyes off of me. My arm jerked up as fire burst in a violent stream in her chest. She toppled backwards, shrieking as the flames covered her chest and arms, spreading faster than I'd ever seen it.

"Now *that* was a truly stupid move, Essie," Chase's voice loomed overhead. I looked up into the pitch black top of the tent in shock as dozens of demons dropped down from the ceiling, each one exactly like the one I had seen in my dream. "You made me go and use my new little pet on you."

"Come out and show your face!" I screamed as the demons charged for me claws extended. I ran over to Kayden's frozen form and did the first thing that came to mind. Shoving my hand onto his face, I set him on fire too.

The effect was instant. Kayden screamed, exploding into smoke. The second he re-formed he started to swear at me until he saw the others heading our way. I didn't need to tell him that if they took a hold of me, everything would be over.

Kayden opened his mouth and exploded again into black smoke, trailing through the whole room. People started to stir, instantly recoiling and screaming in horror as they took in the sight of a burning corpse and demons scrambling about.

A figure blocked my sight of the demons and smoke, Chase's newly mangled form even more grotesque than when he'd been alive. He gave me his best dagger-toothed smile before reaching out and wrapping his hands around my throat.

"Let her go!" A familiar voice soared from above. Abigail swung her feet into Chase's face, sending him flying into a crowd of screaming people. She landed with grace and pulled out four sharp ninja stars from thin air, flinging them straight for Chase. "Essallie, get out of here now!"

I didn't need to be told twice. Scrambling up the steps I got halfway there when someone grabbed the back of my dress and punched the back of my spine, hard. Cassie's voice whispered in my ear. "What a weakling. Is that the best you can do, conjure a little firework with your power? Such a sad excuse for Nephilim."

I rolled over to give her a kick in the shins when I saw the silver knife in her hand plunge straight into my rib cage. Pain shot through me and I screamed. Then, for good measure she twisted it. My eyes rolled back into my head as I fought to stay awake.

"Get her out of here!" Someone shouted through the haze. Arms slipped under my shoulders and dragged me up more steps. "It's going to be okay, Essallie, I promise it's going to be okay."

My eyes fluttered open to find Leo hovering above me, eyebrows bunched together in worry. Blood smeared the front of his tuxedo.

"Hope that was a rental," I made a weak joke and gave him my best smile, surprised there wasn't any pain where the knife had gone through my body. I looked down to see blood, lots of it. "I'm so screwed though. Was that really Abigail I saw or did I hallucinate that?"

"I'll tell you later, I promise," Leo gave a weak smile and placed a hand to my cheek then pulled me in for a hug.

"How touching, a last minute embrace." Chase said with mock awe. Claws flung out towards us, each tip covered in venom. I threw my hands out in front of me to create a shield of fire, burning off his claws. Seeing the claws fail he then flung himself straight through the wall of fire, a knife in one hand poised for my heart.

Leo spun me around, keeping me tight in his arms as the blade sunk into his back. He shuddered then collapsed the floor, unmoving.

"Leo!" I shrieked in horror, sinking to the ground and placing my hands over the wound. Blood poured faster than it was supposed to, bubbling and spreading in a smeared pool around him. "Leo, you listen to me. You hold on, god dammit, you hold on. Ursula loves you way too much for you to die like this." I removed my bloody hands from the wound

and cupped his ashen face. "You do not get to die like this."

He opened his mouth and coughed a bubble of blood. "Do you trust me?"

"Yes, yes I do." I sobbed and hugged him closer. I didn't care how much blood I got on my dress, as long as he lived.

Eyes drifting shut, he spoke in the faintest of whispers. "Then go out...there and kick ass. Trust you-yourself because, I trust you..." A final breath escaped his lips. I let out a guttural scream and stood up, shaking from head to toe.

All around the stadium seats and stage floor was a picture of hell. Fire burned in patches as people tried to escape the big top. Demons leap through the packs and slashed at whatever they could consume, Kayden, Abigail, and Ursula all fighting their own set of the demons.

Something inside of me snapped like a rubber band stretched too thin. Rage bubbled under the surface as I looked down to Leo's body and the surrounding chaos. Enough was enough. Fire spread from my hands up and down my body, bathing me in a blinding blue light. I reached further down into my power, a shimmering silhouette of angel wings spreading from my back.

I am Nephilim, created for war, built for destruction.

I sprinted down the steps and sent bursts of flame at any demon that got in the way, incinerating them on the spot and leaving only a puff of brimstone behind. Light bulbs crackled and burst overhead, raining shards of glass. In two smooth jumps I cleared couple of chairs, using the cushions for a little bounce to land right behind Kayden and pierce a demon through the heart.

"About time you opened that vein of magic," Kayden called over his shoulder as he twisted his arm into a makeshift sword, slicing through one of the demons. "What kept you?"

"Where's Chase?" I screamed as I killed two more with a single shot of fire.

"Look up, lovely," Chase shoved his face in front of mine, twisting his smile back to his ears. Grabbing onto my shoulders he flung me into the air and I collapsed onto the small plank of wood connecting the wire in the center to both ends of the tent. Chase balanced on the center of the wire, beckoning me forward.

But I was one step ahead of him. I flung my hands out and released spirals of fire, wrapping it around him as I had with Kayden when we practiced. He only laughed as I drew him in closer and closer until he was hanging right in front of me.

"What a foolish little girl," he sneered with a gleam to his teeth. Already the flames were doing their work of lacing up his body and burning him to death, piece by smoldering piece. "Go ahead and kill me," he said. "You've already marked your own grave with your Watcher lying dead in cold blood."

I tightened my grip on the flames to make them burn more intently. "He wasn't my Watcher. He was my friend, and now he's going to be avenged."

Rather than weep or beg for mercy, Chase laughed. His face was beginning to crumble, breaking off in sharp chunks that sailed to the ground beneath us. "You'll be with me sooner than you know. I hope you like the taste of demon poison because it's spreading through your body *right now.*"

I stared at him, horrified, as he continued to break off in dying chunks. My hands moved down to the stab wound I had received earlier and examined the fabric. Dried blood meshed with new blood, only this time it was darker and starting to sludge. I only had to wait another second before I watched my veins turn black under the skin and overwhelming pain filled my body. I felt myself free fall to the ground and collapse in a screaming heap, my wings having been the only thing that saved me from broken bones. Not that broken bones mattered much when death was trying to break down your door with his steel-tipped boots.

Kayden stabbed the last of the demons and rushed to where I laid, just in time to watch me arch my back and let out a violent, chilling scream. He pinned me down, encasing my thrashing body in an iron-clad grasp. He looked past me to someone else, pleading. "What do I do? Can Nephilim survive this kind of poison?"

I snapped my head to the side to see Ursula and Abigail standing side-by-side, unable to take their eyes off of me. Ursula's dress was torn in several places, dry blood covering half of her face and chest as tears ran down her cheeks. "I don't know," I heard her say to both Kayden and Abigail. "I've never seen it actually used on someone. It's a forbidden poison because of how fast it spreads."

Another scream ripped through my lips, startling the three of them. Abigail reached down and grasped my ankles while Ursula paced back and forth, running her fingers through the mess that was left of her hair. Suddenly she stopped and plunged her hand in-between her breasts, pulling out a small vial of red liquid held around her neck by a thin silver chain. "Here, take this," she said quickly, shaking heavily as she stood in front of him. When he didn't accept it right away she shook even harder. "A- a medicine woman gave it to me years ago. She said I would know when the right time would be to use it."

Kayden reached out and took it, popped off the small cork and poured it down my throat without a second thought. I tried to pin-point the taste, metal and bullets and spray paint all at once, just as I closed my eyes and prayed to wake up in the morning. "For yours and hers sake I hope so."

FIFTEEN
THIS IS WAR

I was dreaming.

Spoils of perfectly cut, fresh grass laid out before me like an evergreen sea. Flowers in the forms of roses and daisies and tulips in every size and color imaginable sprouted up from the dirt, petals in a dance for sunlight. I hadn't the faintest clue of how I'd gotten to such a lovely little meadow and not destroyed it thoroughly but I didn't question it either. For the moment I felt safe, at peace.

Staring up into the endlessly perfect blue sky above I picked a purple rose from the meadow and brought it to my nose, breathing in the fresh, clean scent.

I rolled over on my side to pick another flower when I stopped. Apparently I wasn't the only one in my private field. Kayden laid just liked I did on the ground, hands resting behind his head as he lazily observed the sky above. The second I turned to look at him did he turn to look back at me, an incomprehensible look on his face. Gently he reached out to place a hand on my cheek, resting his cold skin against mine as he sighed.

"Do you know what it means to truly be alone, Essallie?" His voice lingered in the air like smoke in a parlor room.

I came up with a dozen different retorts, each one more wounding to his ego than the last. Yet I found I didn't want to say them; instead, I just wanted to stare into his eyes. We lingered there, his question hanging in the silence for an immeasurable amount of time. His eyes burned into mine, the muddy brown turning into an enchanting hazel, shimmering like a desert in the sweltering heat. Inside each other's eyes, we exchanged tales of our pain. I was surprised to see just how much his hurt echoed my own.

"I think you already know the answer to the question at hand, Kayden," I whispered, the smallest smile I could manage on my lips. Slowly my eyes started to shut, my head lowering as the darkness began to swallow me whole. All around me my dream began to flicker as my subconscious fought to keep it alive. Another hand pressed on my free cheek, the shock from the sudden intensive cold pressure bringing me back to my dream for but a moment.

"Essallie, you need to stay with me. Just for a little while longer," Kayden whispered with a strong tone.

As much as I wanted to agree and stay with him in a perpetual dream-land forever, suspended in time, the darkness was coaxing me with a better offer. Everything around me felt so comfortable, so warm and soothing.

My eyelids fluttered. "Why?" I mumbled, my voice thick with sleep.

A hand ran through my hair as I heard a soft chuckle echo around me. "Because I am a foolish demon, driven by desire."

"I don't think that's foolish," my whisper was barely audible as I fought to stay awake. It felt like weights were trying to keep my eyelids down, but I strained against them so I could see his face one more time before sinking back into sleep. "I call that bravery, or ballsy."

This time when my eyes opened, I knew it wasn't just another dream. My body had a dull ache to it, the kind that told me that somehow I had managed to survive to see another day. That, and because Kayden was sitting at my bedside looking like he hadn't slept for several days straight.

"Hey," I said hoarsely, and immediately winced at the sound of it. I tried to swallow but it felt exposed and raw. "It's all good. I'm still alive."

Kayden snapped up from his chair with enough force to rocket off to the moon. His eyes were a bright brown as he stared at my face for a moment before breaking into the hugest, most awkward smile I think I'd ever seen on him.

"What," he began. "Is your freaking malfunction? I've been sitting here for nearly two days thinking I was going to have to call your brother and make up some wild excuse that magically turned you comatose." He sank into the cushioned tan chair that matched the bedroom decor of wherever we were with a grand sigh. "At least now I can take you home in one piece."

Every inch of me felt like I'd been kicked in and rolled around in a bucket of glass shards for good measure. Somehow I was still able to smile. "Where the heck are we, anyway?"

"Charon's Hospital. It was only a block away once we cleared everyone out of the tent. No one really noticed your super-saiyan transformation, too. Mostly everyone just wanted to know if you were dead or alive."

A small, tentative knock came from across the room. Ursula stepped in, visibly uncomfortable, and handed Kayden a coffee. She gave me the faintest of nods before promptly turning around and exiting faster than girls moving in on sale items.

"What's wrong with her?" I asked in a clipped tone, then immediately thought of Leo. "Is Leo-?"

Kayden nodded, his expression turned grim. "He was just one of a dozen or so that were gravely injured and killed, yourself included. If it wasn't for," he trailed off, eyes looking back to the door frame. "If it wasn't for really good timing, you wouldn't be alive right now."

I thought about Jayson dressed in his Sunday best, sobbing over my casket, and shuddered. One of my hands reached up to touch the pendant that still hung around my neck. "He said he was my Watcher," I tried to not let my voice break. "That it was all coming back to him just before the circus performance. What if he was?"

He looked down to the ground below to advert my gaze. "If he really was, then it means you'll die. Not today or tomorrow, but soon."

My stomach sank even further. "There's only one way to find out," I said with a hard face. "I'll have to check my birth certificate for the time on it. Here, help me out of bed."

"Uh, how about no?" He stood up and gently pushed me back down onto the bed. "You've still got poison running through your system. Healers said it would take another day of rest before it would all clear from your blood."

I sat up again, pushing against him. "Look, I so do not want your pity party and sympathy bullshit. The fever was worse than this." I swung both legs over to the side of the bed and did a test wiggle of the feet and toes before I made an attempt to stand.

"You know he's right," a male voice said from the doorway. "You could re-draw the venom back into your system if you keep that up. Then it'll go back down to having only one Nephilim on the planet again."

Kayden and I both looked over at the same time, no doubt to say something rude, only to stop. The man in the doorframe looked around my age, maybe a little older. His hair was a bright, brilliant platinum blonde identical to Ursula's, and his teal colored eyes instantly reminded me of a stormy sky. Dressed in a brown leather jacket, jeans and a oil smudged t-shirt he looked like someone who came in with the tumbleweeds and stepped out kicking ass and taking names.

"Wait a minute," I held up a hand and bit back a wince. "Did you just say Nephilim?"

A raw, edgy smile came to his lips. "Yes ma'am. It's about time I found you, Essallie. My name is Ari, and we're the start of the army."

READ ON FOR A PREVIEW OF

OBUMBRATE

| BOOK TWO IN THE ILLUMINE SERIES |

PROLOGUE
THUNDER

In one second, everything can change.

Life can bloom like a flower, exposing petals of a raw and unyielding beauty. Death can touch and silence a voice, leaving an abyss in place of a familiar soul.

Gripping the steering wheel of her car, Bethanie knew all too well how precious time was. It was a fickle thing, working against her in ways she had only ever seen as a curse, aimed to destroy her lone chances at redeeming herself in her short life. Her foot pressed harder against the gas pedal, wheels tearing through the thick and muddy back roads as it poured relentlessly.

Against the back of her mind, she knew it didn't make much sense to be driving in the madness of the weather. Rain pounded at the windshield, making it virtually impossible to see anything before her. Yet the continuing *tick-tock* of the silver pocket watch resting on her lap reminded her that she had a place to be, a place she would never reach in time.

Once again, time was working against her.

She closed her eyes for one gratifying moment, perfectly

recalling the hands that had given her the silver pocket watch. Hands that belonged to someone she had spent all her life trying to get close to, desperate to admit the way his skin electrified hers. Desperate to say how much she ached to know the taste of his lips. Desperate to hear her name leave his tongue until time robbed him of the ability to speak. Desperate to hear that iconic message, three little words that could make or break a heart.

Lightning blazed through the sky, illuminating the world in a hazy blue-tinted glow. It was then that she saw the familiar back of an old, yellow car, that her heart stopped.

She pulled over to the side, her door thrown open before the car had come to a complete stop. Her chest tightened at the sight spread before her; car lights still on, driver door hanging wide open, all the signs of something terrible, but no body to prove it.

Bethanie scrambled around the car, ignoring her slip of feet and short-lived crash in the growing mud puddles. He was here, she could feel it. Her eyes started to search around the road and field of crops, when she spotted a parting in the field.

She ran, sprinting and screaming into the waist high spread, spotting his body only a dozen feet in. He lay eagle-spread, eyes vacant and unmoving as they stared into the swirling black mass hanging in the sky.

"*No!*" She screamed louder, dropping to her knees beside the freshly dead corpse. She grabbed at his arms, shoulders, chest, and face, anything to bring a response out of the boy she had carelessly wander from her sight.

Smacking at his face once more with rattled hands, her screams continued. "You don't get to die like this, not here, not now. You have a bigger cause. Do you hear me? You do not *get to die.*"

In that moment, everything stopped.

Like a tear in time, the world seemed to pause on itself, waiting for the push to move forward. She looked around, tears still running over her cheeks, waiting for a sign, a charge she could react to. Overhead the sky rumbled, the crackling of thunder the only thing creating sound other than her.

Bethanie fished for something against her chest, finding a small brass key woven entirely from wire. With a kiss, she placed it on his chest, then wrapped herself around the boy's limb body.

A cold draft rushed over the small clip of field, a twisting sensation starting in Bethanie's chest. Icicles collected on the tips of the grass, a veil of snow gathering on her shoulders and hair, as her once damp tears turned sharp and solid on her face. With a final breath, she exhaled those three powerful words to the chilled body beneath her.

And lightning struck them both.

ONE
BREAK ME DOWN

Once upon a time, on a cold winters night
A young and fair maiden was given a fright
She had awoken to chaos beyond her control
A horrorful sight, a new world to behold
The ocean sealed under a mass of chains
While perched atop, one coffin remains
A circlet of fire wrapped about like a cage
As muffled screams sounded desperate with rage
Yet the only comfort the maiden received
Was watching the white roses burn as she grieved

"Miss Hanley."

I jolted against my plastic-backed chair, muscles clenched. The pencil in my hand froze mid-stroke as my mind went blank. I dared the chance to look up. Mr. Whitley, my Biology teacher, gave me a disapproving stare, lips pulled tightly across his aged face. Behind him, my classmates all stared at me, stone-cold silence filling the room.

Instantly I relaxed. A man like Whitley was about as threatening as a newborn hamster. I kept a cool face as I asked, "Was there something you needed?"

Behind him, I heard some of the kids snicker. Whitley did his best to appear intimidating, puffing out his chest and letting his glasses dangle precariously on the edge of his nose, but only succeeded in looking like a moth-eaten teddy bear. "I was going to commend you on your excellent note-taking for the final next week. Thankfully, I held my tongue." His hand rested lightly on the edge of my desk, tapping it twice at the paper on my desk. "It *is* good to know though, that you won't be failing your art final."

I glanced down at the paper in front of me. A large human eye encompassed the whole sheet from corner to corner, dark lashes framing a detailed interior sketch of chains settling over ocean waves, a sole hand reaching out from under the surface. Above the chains rested a coffin white roses lain on top, fire licking around the base. It was a scene straight from a macabre book.

"Uh, thanks? The idea sort of stemmed from a poem, I think." I half-shrugged, not really sure where I got the idea from. Whitley didn't seem to notice, or care for that matter.

"I'd put the drawings away and lay off the Edgar Allen Poe, Miss Hanley. You missed a lot while daydreaming away. Unless your wish is to have my class again next year, your peers all off at college, leaving you behind in this tiny town," he straightened and moved his hand off my desk, returning up to the white board at the front, continuing to map out the portions of our upcoming final.

Tugging the sleeves of my cream sweater over my hands, I tried to focus on the board in front of me. My eyes however, had another plan. They continued to drift down to the drawing laid out before me. It was one of dozens I had completed in the last two weeks, each one more detailed than the last. It always started with the same almond eye shape; same curve of the pencil under my hand, same smudging and detailing, everything perfectly identical, save for one thing. Some of the eyes told stories of black birds and blood, others told stories of sunlight and fire. The aching part was that each had been created while I revisited Leo's death in my mind.

I snapped my notebook shut to hide the drawings out of sight. Lips clenched tight, I made sure to pay extreme attention to the white board and write down as much as I could before the bell rang ten minutes later. Whitley seemed pleased when I passed by him to leave, apparently taking my sudden interest in last-minute note-taking was on his accord. Maybe he thought I'd taken his words seriously, like the notion of having to repeat a year in a public education system was the most terrifying thing that could happen to me.

Hah. If only he knew. One look in my head and he'd see school was one of the last good blessings I had left.

In the hallway I stood in front of my open locker, staring at its contents without really seeing. I half-pretended to debate on what books would be most important to take home with me for studying, but what exactly mattered when you knew death was knocking on your door? Even if I did give a damn, I could still fail all of my finals and graduate with a low C-average in every class. I had to give it to my grandparents. If it hadn't been for them pushing me into one of NYC's select private schools, I wouldn't have the luxury of slacking off like I had been. Again, that was still assuming it meant something. The idea of even seeing graduation rested on the assumption that I'd live long enough to actually make it down the aisle and take that diploma, that maybe they'd teach me something useful for my limited existence. Seeing as they didn't teach me the ins and outs of being half of a mythical creature, and how to save myself from a fiery death, I was betting that would never happen.

Nothing had gone right since I'd set foot in Belfast. And that was putting it lightly. Just as I has started to settle into my old home I had learned a bitter truth; that every part of my life had been a sick, crafted lie. From the second I came into existence, I had been shuffled and shoved, picked on by a lunatic mother, abandoned by an unimaginable, alleged heavenly being of a father. I had learned that running from your past only brings it front and center, hungry with a vengeance. Life, to me, felt like a tragic painting. I felt like a sparrow with clipped wings, still believing it could fly.

I sighed and pressed my forehead to my locker. Since coming home from the hospital in Charon, day to day life had been practically impossible. It was hard enough learning I wasn't the human I thought I was, but add in a demon that was constantly looking for a weak-point in my instinctive defenses to kill me, and I was already in over my head. Kayden, Ursula, and Abigail had all agreed to let the past fall behind us and to never speak of it again. Leo wasn't dead to anyone but us, and as far as everyone else knew he was off in New Zealand for a student exchange program.

Leo... he was gone. Everything had happened so fast, my mind was still trying to wrap itself around the reality of it. A cold shiver raised goosebumps on my skin, scattered fragments of that night playing out in my head. One minute, it had been about dressing up and having fun, embracing a side of me I didn't know was possible to love.

Then it had all turned to blood, so much blood.

Blood on my hands, dark red liquid staining my palms, embedding itself deep in the cracks and cuticles of my fingers. Blood on my white dress and on Leo's button-up, sticky and slick as it clung to his paling skin, clouded eyes staring blankly at the ceiling as his final breath exhaled from his lips.

I wanted to mourn him, honor his death, but everywhere I turned someone was watching me. Kayden rarely left my side at school, and when I would think I'm alone at home the floorboards would creak and give away Jayson silently listening in to my stifled sobs. Jayson quickly caught on that something was different when I came home from what he thought had been an innocent sleepover at Ursula's. Maybe it had been the way I started sobbing the first time I picked up my sketchbook, days after his death. Maybe it had been the night he found me sobbing on the bathroom floor, my hands scrubbed raw to the point of bleeding all over the linoleum floor. He had silently been watching me fall to pieces, completely unaware of the weight on my shoulders, completely unaware of how I wanted to tell him everything. Instead I had lied, citing that finals was taking a toll on me, that Abigail would know exactly how to help. After all, she was my shoulder to lean on.

Too bad Abigail wasn't an option.

It may have been only two weeks since Chase nearly succeeded in killing me again, but his violent attack left only a fraction of the sting Abigail's words had. By the time I noticed she had been in the hospital by my side the entire time, I had thought I was delusional. How could a mortal be in a mythical realm? She was human, or so I had assumed.

Fool me once, shame on me. Fool me twice, shame on me twice as hard.

A light cough came off from my left, my eyes spotting an unmistakable pair of Doc Martens standing next to me. "Are you coming down to lunch today?"

I shut my locker, wiggling the handle to make sure it was locked. I made sure not to look at her as I passed her to make my way down the hall. "I'd rather not, Abigail." I winced as her name passed my lips.

Abigail followed behind me, her long peasant skirt making

169

swishing sounds against the sides of her legs. "Essallie, it's been two weeks. Enough is enough." She tried to match my stride as I walked faster until she couldn't take it. Hands grabbed at my sweater and turned me around. "So I'm a little weird, like you didn't already know. If it makes you feel better, I'll say I'm sorry."

"That's just it, Abby. I didn't." My eyes began to prickle, tears threatening to make a show. But I couldn't cry, not with several students still in the hallway with us. I shook my head. I felt like an overused bleeding heart, shocked to life too many times to count. "I can't accept your half-assed apology. You're not sorry you kept everything from me because it was 'good for me'. You're sorry you were ousted. You could have told me."

Abigail pursed her lips. I watched her lip curl upward as her trademark sneer and eye-roll made its appearance. "What did you think, Essie? That we became such fast friends because we connected so well?" She paused and tucked a stray piece of dark red hair behind her ear, deafening silence pounding between us. When she spoke, it was quiet and low. "I didn't mean it like that."

"Then tell me how you did mean it." I fought to control the volume of my voice. My fingers began to twitch as I fought the need to let my knees buckle from the quivering that ran rampant in my joints. "You know, I'm not some fragile little thing that's too delicate to hear the truth. I should have known anyone who was close to me was bound to be tired to my freakish side."

"I wanted to tell you, I really did." Abigail still spoke in a low-tone. "But it wasn't my call."

Red began to bleed into my sight, clouding my view. Every beat of my heart matched the pounding in my head. I spoke in a hiss. "Of course not. It's never your call. It's always someone else's. I'm sorry I ever trusted you, ever knew you." I rocked back on my heels and reached up to press my fingers against my temples. "God, why is every freaking person around me some kind of supernatural *freak?*" My voice cracked at the end, and I lost my hold on the scream built in the back of my throat.

It was only the two of us now, all the other students having shuffled off and away from the scene we- I was making.

"Listen-"

"No, *you* listen. I don't want to hear your sob story of how you kept me in the dark for my own protection. This isn't some stupid vampire novel where everyone keeps the squishy little human from knowing anything." Fire sparked on my fingertips, a familiar dull ache spreading through my veins. I wanted to release it, let the full force consume the hallway and both of us in it. "I can set anyone on fire in a given moment, burn forests to the ground, reduce buildings to ash! Is that why you couldn't tell me anything? Because I'm like a Molotov cocktail?"

Abigail moved to answer, but I shoved a flaming finger centimeters away from her face, silencing her with a gasp for air. "No more lies, Abigail. You're going to tell me everything, or nothing will stop me from setting you ablaze."

"It wasn't her choice, Essallie. It was mine," Kayden's voice called from the end of the hallway. I looked up to see him approach us, each step bringing his shifting silhouette into sharper focus. His dark black hair spiked on his head stood in sharp contrast to his rich tanned skin, eyes a spinning mist of hazel and black. Even dressed in an everyday get up of a windbreaker, t-shirt and jeans he looked like a dark immortal, the kind of person you'd swoon over under the bleachers and dreamt about at night. If I hadn't known better I'd have called him seductive, cunning, a mystery I'd long to find more about.

Eyes locked on Kayden, he stopped as a brilliant arc of

flames erupted on my second hand, engulfing it whole. It spun into a ball and cradled in my palm as I held it in his direction. "You stay out of this. I'll pick my battle with you next, *demon*." I gave him a piercing stare. He had been someone to trust, to tell me everything and help me navigate this new power I could barely contain. Instead, it felt like he'd thrown me to the wolves. My attention moved back to Abigail. "Who else is weird like me, like us? My brother? Thomas? Jessica?"

Abigail took a step backward, hesitation written across her face. She stole a quick glance at Kayden, who shook his head silently.

"Oh my God. Jessica?" I hissed. "Is that why she's still in Portland? Did she even *go* to Portland?"

"I can't say."

"Dammit Abigail!"

Like flipping on a switch, fire shot from my hands. A wall of bright blue flame instantly separated them from me, my fire acting like a barricade. Abigail reacted in barely enough time; stumbling into the lockers behind, her she quickly put out the fire that started on the hem of her skirt. Kayden silently joined her, swirls of black smoke curling at his feet.

"How am I to know anything you tell me is what's really going on? Or am I just supposed to trust you both, the demon and the sneak, both holding your own goals at heart," I hissed, backing down the hall to make for the exit to the parking lot.

"Essie, this is enough. You can't keep doing this," Kayden snapped as he stood alongside Abigail. "This is what it's like being different, you have to accept that. People live and people die. Leo was only the beginning. The sooner you accept that, the sooner we can plan."

I felt a stab at my heart as he said Leo's name aloud. He shouldn't have been allowed to speak that name, the name of that brilliant life I let die. Grief washed over me in waves that was almost too painful to hold back. The urge to let fire engulf the whole hall crossed my mind again. "Plan for what? How much more have you kept from me? I can't trust either of you, not after what happened." I turned to face Abigail, fighting the urge to cry again. "Was any of our friendship real? Or was Kayden using you to get to me from the beginning?"

Abigail turned her gaze to Kayden and started to speak. He instantly drowned her out, eyes never left my face. "By all means, get even more pissed. Blow yourself up and kill everyone here. It'll be their blood on your hands. You think Leo's death was hard, try living with the knowledge you killed hundreds."

I looked down to my blazing hands, watching the fire roll over my skin harmlessly. "You know what? I like the sound of that." I flexed my fingers, letting coils of the flame lash out at them from the blaze between us. With the pressure of my body I launched the wall straight at them. Kayden wrapped himself around Abigail as she screamed just as the fire raced around Kayden, burning him in seconds. It dawned on me that Kayden could be gone from that burst, or that Abigail could be burned to the point of deformity, maybe even death. Yet somehow, I didn't care. Every feeling I had was locked in a box within my soul, leaving me with a hollow sensation I couldn't place.

Spinning sharply on my heels, I crossed the parking lot and slid inside my car. The growing roar of the engine felt oddly satisfying, the rumble just enough to match the quakes and quivers of my body. For a second I looked back to the building, my neck tilted to see inside the doors where I had abandoned the two traitors. My car had just inched past the double glass doors when I spotted a burst of black smoke fill the hallway.

The skin on my knuckles flared white against the steering wheel as I navigated through the streets of Belfast. I was searching for something, anything to distract me from setting fire to the whole town. School was too risky, too many potential events that could trigger my anger and hurt someone innocent. Home was just as dangerous, as Jayson was bound to ask me why I was so uptight, and I didn't want to hurt him. I was barely keeping my temper in check as I drove, and I knew that at any point I could lose it and blow up the car. I needed some place quiet, somewhere the fresh air could hit my lungs and tame my thoughts with a gentle breeze.

I crossed past the same church three times over before I settled on parking. It was mid-afternoon, so no services were being held. I made sure to pull my sketchbook from my messenger bag before I left the car. Connected to the small church was an equally small graveyard, the perfect place to go for a quiet moment. After all, who's quieter than the dead?

Only the sound of my footsteps sounded around me as I rounded the headstones one by one. Most of them were faded, crumbling from age and weather, and the new ones stood out in sharp contrast. My fingertips brushed over the black marble of a new headstone naming an older woman who had died four years ago. Instantly I was enraged. Leo deserved one of these, he deserved to be buried and rest. But the stupid facade Kayden and his parents agreed to all put on made that impossible. All because no one wanted to cause a panic in the town.

Between the hospital and home I had learned there was much more to the eyes of Leo than anyone had let on. His family held a key role in gate-keeping the entrances to Charon. They decided when new entrances could be placed and who held control over them for safe passage. Leo had been the last of his blood line. Now, with him gone, the question was who would take over when his parents pass.

Finding space between two aged headstones, I found a comfortable place on the grass to sit, my sketchbook propped up on my legs for support. Slowly I turned the pages, taking cursory glances over the abstract designs. It used to be something I loved, an outlet for my frustration. Now all I saw was Leo. Images of his hands reaching for my pencil, his happy smile as he showed me Charon, it all blurred behind a wall of haze in my mind. I had it shut it out- all of it -if I was to ever function again. So much easier said than done when you've seen two violent deaths before your eyes.

My fingers found the pencil I kept in the ringed binding and before I knew it, I was drawing. Sheer impulse drove the pencil against paper, framing a beautiful almond-shaped eye with a dark iris, small arcs of light breaking through the black smudges of lead. It wasn't an eye I openly recognized. Most of my drawings were normally manga related; cartoon eyes with dramatic eyelashes and open messages displayed in their large stare. This one was human, a real life eye.

"I didn't know you enjoyed my gaze that much, Nephilim." A female voice softly purred behind me. Instantly I snapped out of my haze, like breaking through a watery surface with force. I looked around to see the graveyard had turned darker, shadows pulling towards the headstones and swirling around me. Slowly they spun upward, framing in a delicate woman I had only met once.

I waited for the initial shock of wear off before I used my voice. The Queen looked as ornate and elegant as she had the night of the circus disaster. A flowing gown of the blackest of fabrics cut with a sweetheart top swallowed her petite frame. Gloves of the same fabric were decorated with sparkling pearls and Swarovski crystals. Beautifully dressed or not, it was her pale face framed by curtains of black hair that stood out. "Your gaze?"

She glided over with inhuman grace and gently crouched down to point at the picture I had been working on. "Correct me if I'm wrong, but I believe that would be my eye." She stared at me with curiosity. "Do you carry the Sight, as well?"

I stared up at her face and back to the photo. Sure enough, the photo I had been instinctively scribbling had been of her eyes. Maybe I was psychic? More likely than not I had remembered her face in my subconscious when I was revisiting that night in my memories. Then again, it wouldn't be the first time I was surprise by my own hidden abilities.

I shrugged and brushed off her question. I was in no mood to deal with any kind of mind games she might try to enact on me. "Did you need something? Or do you just enjoy taking afternoon strolls in the mortal realm?"

The Queen appeared unfazed by my cold shoulder. "Kayden said you were brash. I can see he was right." She smiled. "Do you speak to him like this as well?"

"You answer my question, and I'll answer yours."

Her smile faltered by a fraction before she recovered with poised grace. "Very well, then. I came to see you. You had left in such haste after the... incident. I was worried for your well being."

Her lies lingered in the air like bitter puffs of sulfur, strong enough to taste, strong enough to gag on. "Two weeks is an awfully long time to wait. You could have just been honest and said you wanted to see if I was dead yet."

She opened her mouth slightly to speak, only to close it. Rich honey brown eyes narrowed at me. "You haven't answered my question, Nephilim."

"Essallie. It's Essallie," I corrected with a snap.

"Essallie it is, then. You haven't answered my question."

I turned my eyes back to the drawing on my lap. With a jerk of the paper, I ripped it from the sketchbook, crumbled it into a wad and chucked over my shoulder.

"Only those who smell to high heavens of bullshit and ulterior motives." I rose to my feet and faced her, heat lancing through my veins like spears ready for the fight. "Spit it out.

You didn't come here to check on me. So why are you here?"

Her eyes widened in surprise as I stood there, waiting. After today's nonsense with Abigail and Kayden, I had heard enough bullshit to span my lifetime six times over. Queen or no Queen, I didn't owe her anything. If anything, she owed me her life. It had been my hands covered in Chase's blood, not hers. For sacrificing my own lifespan to a torture of burning veins so her and all her little supernatural freaks could continue on in their meaningless existence.

Finally, she spoke. "You're smart. Smart enough to know not to trust me." Brushing past me, I watched as the shadows moved with her, forming a small pool around the hem of her dress. "I am, however, surprised to see you trust a demon of all things. Especially someone like Kayden."

It was bait, I knew it. She was testing to see if I'd wait to see the shoe drop off the other foot. Fire spread from my fingers and washed over my hands. I pointed an emblazoned finger at her. "Your simple mind tricks won't work on me. I'm not interested in playing your petty game."

A horrid smile spread so far across her face, I thought it might split in half. She laughed as she stepped closer, until all I could see was the kohl lining the rims of her narrowed eyes. "Oh, you'll play my game whether you like it or not."

God, she sounded like a freaking cartoon villain. I started to turn and leave, my hands still engulfed in the angelic flame. "Sure thing, Queenie."

Shadows erupted from the ground, bursting skyward in sharp, jagged spikes. They spiraled together until a thick black cocoon sealed around the graveyard. I pushed a burst of flame through my veins to light up the inside when I saw a glimmering black spear launch into my hand. I screamed and the shadows launched into a fury, dozens of them stabbing at my hands, my arms, anywhere the fire pulsed from my body.

As I screamed and thrashed, the Queen spoke. "You see,

Essallie, there isn't an option to ignore my voice. When you control the dark and all its splendor, you'll find many are willing to listen if it means their lives will be spared, if but for a moment."

Pressure crushed my chest as I fought to breathe. Breathy whispers spoke to me, like wind whistling through barren tree tops. My fire was gone, swallowed by the stabbing shadows that sunk into every inch of me. Emptiness seeped into my pores and filled me with a hollow sensation. Everything was so dark, so empty, so lost.

The shadows retreated, and I collapsed onto the ground. I watched through watery eyes as they took their place just under the Queen, shifting and swirling. She reached down and ran her hand across the shadows in a loving gesture. Some of them had spun up and into the fabric of her gown, forming swirls of deep violet against the black. "Now, let's chat."

I unsteadily rose to my feet, every inch of my body shaking. I felt like a leaf in the wind- powerless, frail, empty. The burn inside of my veins was gone, cooled to an bitter icy sensation that spread throughout my body. I reached deep inside to trigger the fire only to find a cold hollow instead. My fire was gone.

"What," my voice cracked. "What did you do to me?"

The corners of her lips hitched into the vague image of a smile. She breezed past me to sit on a thick headstone several rows over. Her hand beckoned me to follow. "Teenagers these days, " I heard her say. "Always so eager to start a fight. No doubt the hormones compel you to do it." Sitting on the etched granite, she looked up at me with a sympathetic gaze. "It must be hard, being so young and having this power you can barely control. I almost wish I could relate."

I stared down to my shaking, open hands. Hormones were the least of my worries. When you played with fire, you were bound to be burned. She could never understand, no matter how tied to her magic she was. "You don't know anything about this. Just go, leave me alone."

She let out a barely audible laugh. "You underestimate my ability to feel. Most demons lose their ability to harness emotion after centuries of seclusion from humanity, but there are a small few who never forget. I know more than you'll ever understand, Essallie." I looked up in time to watch her face harden, her mouth set into a thin line. Something stirred behind her eyes. "Some of us experience things that can never be erased. You think it was painful watching a friend die-"

"He wasn't a friend. He was so much more than I'll ever be able to explain," I spoke faster than I could think, the words rolling off my tongue with violent force. My hands shook as I missed the comfort of my inner fire. "Everyone keeps telling he was someone I barely knew, had little time with, and because of that I'm supposed to get over his death just like everyone else. They don't understand. When he died, it felt like part of me went with him. This goes deeper than some friend dying, this was someone tied to my soul."

For a moment, the Queen stayed silent. Only the subdued sound of her shadows filled the empty space between us. "I lost a daughter. So yes, I do know what it is like to lose a part of your soul, your spirit, or whatever it is we supernaturals have inside us. I know what it's like to feel yourself rip in half." A haunted look stirred in her eyes as she spoke through a thin lipped smile. "She looked just like you. That's why the night at the circus I was so guarded. I had thought for sure that my mind was trying to do me in."

My stomach dropped into my feet the same moment my chest let off a jolt of pain. Embarrassment and humiliation washed over me in waves. Here I stood, complaining over someone who may or may not have been tied to my soul, and yet she harbored a deeper secret than I had. A daughter, someone of true flesh and blood, lost to the ashes and dust.

The image of a jackass came to mind. I didn't linger on the thought for long, but I did add the loss of her daughter to the list of things Kayden had failed to fill me in with. And that list was growing awfully damn fast.

"Kayden never mentioned anything like that." I gently replied. I wasn't sure what to say past that. I'm sorry your daughter died and I'm pissing and moaning over a boy? My apologies I'm a selfish hot-headed teenager?

The lack of apology didn't seem to faze the Queen. A faint smile tugged at her lips as she let out a huff of laughter. "I can see Kayden hasn't told you nearly as much as you think he has. Tell me, what did he say about me?"

That she was cruel. Anyone who got on her bad side was as good as dead. All the things you'd tell someone to keep them from speaking to another. "Nothing redeeming."

She nodded, running a hand through her hair and twirling the ends around her index finger. "What reason does he have for staying by your side?"

"What do you mean?"

"I simply find it a little odd," she began, speaking slow to my narrowed gaze. "I've known Kayden for over seven hundred years, and not once has he been the type to simply stay with a fledgling, a newcomer, unless there was something to be gained."

But I knew what was keeping him. I was the only one with the key to his freedom. My still-beating heart ensured his connection to me, our uncanny bond. As long as I lived and breathed, he would continue to remain in the shadows, waiting for his chance to finish the charge assigned to him.

"I think he was wrong." I heard her say, surfacing me from my thoughts. When I looked up at her, she was shaking her head. "You don't seem to be easily manipulated. Then again, I didn't kiss you like he had."

For the second time today, I felt the air leave my lungs.

My mind instantly brought me back images of his molten gaze, the smooth sound of his voice. I banished the pictures from my mind and ignored the heat on my face. That was supposed to have been our private moment. I hadn't told anyone of the kiss. "How- how do you know about that?"

"Essallie, do not tell me that you thought that kiss was real." The Queen came down to my level, swaths of black fabric and energy-hungry shadows licking at the edge of my feet. She stared at me intently. "I can see it in your eyes and the red on your cheeks. You're fond of him."

Fever in the form of blush colored my cheeks, my heart beating to the tune of a painful pitter-patter. "Answer me! Who told you about the kiss?"

"Who else would have told me, but the demon who did it himself."

I was starting to think my gut-punch reaction to everything I had learned recently was becoming a habit. Forcing myself to keep breathing, I ran my hands through my hair. Anything to keep myself from trying to punch a decade-old headstone.

The Queen continued, her face carefully kept neutral. "He had laughed and told me I hadn't to worry about you. That any chance of you ascending was gone because of a *little magic* he'd done before you had all arrived." She frowned as she spoke, no doubt from seeing the physical pain I was struggling to keep inside the more she revealed. "No war could come from a dying angel, he'd said."

"He, he said he would help me." A curious numbing sensation began to spread from my chest to my fingertips. He had offered to help, that he would make it fair before trying to kill me. That's what was supposed to make this interesting. But if he'd purposely made me focus on him instead of Leo... if I had never kissed Kayden, would Leo and I have connected? Would he still be here, guiding me, saving me

181

from myself?

"I'm sorry, but I need to go," I said, standing on my shaking limbs. The numbing sensation was starting to turn into sharp jabs of cold, sinking deep into my gut and heart. "I'm sorry about your daughter."

She held out a hand to stop me, but didn't grab or push at me. "Don't you want your gift back? Your fire?"

I shivered and stared at the ground. A bitter taste coated my tongue when I spoke. "Probably not. Unless you're giving me the okay to kill Kayden."

The Queen came to stand before me, mere inches left between us. Hands cupped just under her chest, she gently extended them outward toward me, a small blue flame flickering in her palm. It shot straight for my chest, lancing into me with instant effect. Warmth spread through every inch of my body, replacing the numbing, hollow sensation that had been there moments ago.

"You may leave," the Queen said. "but before you do, a warning. Kayden is not a person to be trusted. He'll only use you for his own gain in the end."

"Like I didn't already know."

"And one more thing. Do be careful." Her voice sounded almost resembled something of sympathy and genuine concern. "When it comes to the race of Nephilim, the world reacts in two ways. None will take kindly to your angelic blood; there will be those who will seek to harvest your blood for their own gain. Others will want you dead, no matter the cost."

Wariness crept over my skin. "Why would you tell me this?"

"Because one of the last Nephilim was killed at the hands of a madwoman. A woman who tried to harvest the blood of Nephilim to create the perfect race."

READ ON FOR A PREVIEW OF

a shard
of ice

A BLACK SYMPHONY NOVEL

.1.
UNCHAINED MELODY

The bitter, pinching wind stung the Captain's face as he perched against the glacial-coated bars lining the ship. Even in the twenty plus years of fishing, the sight of his vessel transforming into an icy death trap never failed to mystify him. Hunks of ice, rigid and sharp, weighed everything down onto the deck and its contents, forming a near-impenetrable barrier over it all.

Then again, that was what you got when you sailed a fishing boat through the untamable sea.

He stepped back inside, closing the door tightly behind him and making down the tiny, narrow hall. Voices and light danced ahead, rousing shouts and cheers as chips and other random items were scattered onto a small table crammed in the middle of a tightly wedged room.

"Ice has got to be ten feet thick, easily. Looks like we're here for the night, boys," he said with a half-hearted shrug. A round of grunts and groans ran across the small room. Six

184

men of varying ages had squeezed themselves about the table, shoulders and arms draped in thick wool in a vain attempt to shield their skin from the bitter elements lurking outside.

Shoulders bunched, one of the older men sitting in the far corner reached up to scratch the scruff lining his jaw. He shrugged with displacement. "Only means more time for Jesse here to lose his wife in a game of cards."

The men laughed, save for a slightly younger one who'd gone red in the face. His voice came out in a half-strangled squeak. "You wouldn't know what to do with her even if you did win her with your crappy hand."

Resisting the urge to roll his eyes, the Captain started to shuffle his way about the small space. He paused at the door frame leading to their bunks, glancing over his shoulder. Seated alongside the frame on a metal folding chair, the youngest of their new recruits was quiet and unmoving. Tuffs of slightly curling blonde hair peeked from under his ratty skullcap sporting a hole in the back.

The Captain placed a hand on the kid's shoulder, frowning as he stiffened to the touch. "These rats giving you a hard time, Kyle?"

Leaning back an inch, the boy tilted his head up. Startling, sharp blue eyes glimmered mischievously. He lifted his cards from his chest carefully, exposing a royal flush.

"Not at all, sir," he said quietly. "These rats don't realize a cat is amongst them tonight."

The Captain squinted, confused by the boy's awkward and out-dated choice on words, but laughed it off. Clapping his back, he grinned approvingly. "I remember the first time I-"

A loud bang jolted the ship. Everyone shifted sharply to the left, elbows and shoulders banging into each other as contents from the game spilled onto the crowded floor. The door to the deck flung open, one of the men stampeding inside.

His eyes were wide, swallowing his face. "There's a body, out on the ice."

Disbelief colored the Captain's voice. "What the hell have you been smoking in your pipe?"

The man didn't budge. Green started to creep up his face. "A- a body, outside. On a patch of ice."

Swears and grumbles swelled in the room like a burst of cellos and drums. Several started to gather their chips and coins, while the Captain and two others rose from their seats and made for the door outside. Kyle followed behind, paying little attention to the glacial temperature leeching at his skin joined the small group.

Eyes still wide, the man half-slid across the deck, catching himself on the ice-encrusted railing. He flung an arm out over the metal bars, finger pointed in a wild tremor. "Right there! Between those spikes of ice!"

The few that came out inched closer, exchanging mixed glances. It wasn't uncommon for one of the crew to go crazy every couple of years, in fact they even took bets before shipping off as to who would crack first under the lonely, inky black skies.

Tugging his cap tighter over his ears, Kyle brushed past the Captain, bringing himself alongside the spooked crew member. He squinted, peering into the black expanse marred by faint outlines of craggy ice. Shapes began to take form amidst the dark, spikes of frozen slabs stretching as far as the heavens, like knifes trying to cut into the stars. The jagged pieces cradled a base of perfectly smooth ice, spread like a stage.

Lying in the center, face pressed against the base, lay a girl dressed in a thin white nightgown. Her hair, golden and light, had been fanned out in a perfect circlet around her face.

Kyle felt the color drain from his face, a new chill rattling in his chest that had nothing to do with the cold. Heat raced up his arms, pain prickling at his skin. He winced, breath puffing like little clouds of smoke in front of his face. It couldn't be her...

"Sweet Mary," the Captain gasped, stumbling closer to the rails of the boat. Even against the bitter cold leeching at his body heat, he'd never felt so frozen inside at the sight mapped out in front of him. Staring back at the other men, he screamed. "Don't just stand there, we've got to get them off the ice!"

The Captain's words snapped him out of his haze. Without a moment's pause, the men all moved into action, grabbing ropes and hacking at the ice frantically. Kyle stepped back from the railing, biting his lip. He could feel the etchings on his skin returning to life underneath his sleeves. Her presence alone was enough to trigger the memories, to reawaken the spirit within.

Spinning around, Kyle darted inside the nearest room, grabbing a rope long enough to tether him back to the boat. He looped it around his waist, knotting it and quickly running back onto deck. His fingers shook as he secured the other end to the railing, giving it a final tug to check its hold. Tossing his cap onto the deck, his wild and unruly blonde hair danced around his head like a lion's mane as he jumped from the boat in a single, flawless leap, landing on the ice soundlessly.

He dashed across the slippery ground, gliding to the unconscious girl. For a moment, he stood there, transfixed. Her nightgown was thin and sheer, no where near the proper clothing to be braving the cold the sea. Yet she looked perfect and unharmed. Her skin was a fair peach tint; not a single inch of her skin was damaged by the freezing temperatures. Placing his hands under her, he scooped up the girl's petite frame, cradling her tightly against his chest as he slowly inched his way back to the boat.

Over the railing, he could hear them chanting in symphony, encouraging each other to pull them up from the ice below. Kyle turned down to stare at the girl in his arms, baffled by her calm, placid composure. His fingers gently brushed away at the stray strands of hair covering her face, grazing her skin with his. The gasp and jolt in his chest nearly screamed from his throat. Pictures flooded his mind like a breaking dam, memories so strong he felt reality slipping around him. Sinking his teeth into his lower lip, his clutch tightened to an iron grasp around her immobile frame.

With a final tug, the men hoisted them over the railing and onto the icy deck. Kyle dropped to his side, clutching the girl and covering her head before rolling to his knees, then feet. Closely followed by the four pairs of incredulous stares, he carried her inside the ship, shoving aside the quickly forgotten mugs of beer, coins and unfinished card game to the floor. He placed her on the table delicately, but kept a hand linked in one of hers. She was still warm, her heart beating steady.

Almost instantly, the men all began to fire questions in an uproar.

"How in the hell did she end up all the way out here?"

"There's no other boats but us out here for miles, right?"

"Where are her clothes?"

"How long you think she's been dead?"

"She's not," Kyle spoke with a snap, meeting all eyes with his own steel gaze. "Dead. She has a pulse."

The room went silent. From the end of the room, the Captain pressed forward. His wary eyes went from Kyle's steady gaze to the girl. Her chest rose and fell in tiny spurts.

Glancing over his shoulder, he nodded at the man who first pointed out the body on the ice. "Head on up and radio to base. Tell them we're coming back with a miracle." Scratching his chin, he scowled back at the table. "Will someone get a blanket on her, for crying out loud."

One of the men rustled in the corner, yanking a thin sheet of wool from a folding chair, but Kyle was already removing his worn coat, draping it over the girl. The longer he stared at her, the more he saw it; the familiar shade of gold in her hair, the way her skin seemed to glow on its own, it was all painfully familiar. Memories jabbed at his mind, shocking him to the point of jolting him where he stood. Could it really be her?

"I think I know who she is," he murmured, entranced by her unconscious being. "It's the Morgan girl."

The few men who had stayed paused, silencing any underhanded whispers or suspicions. "She's been missing for weeks, mate. You really think it's her?"

"Only one way to find out," Kyle replied, a sad smile on his face. He stared at her for another moment before taking her back into his arms, making for the narrow hallway to the set of cots they used for beds. "Make sure he tells base that it might be the missing Morgan girl."

They each gave a short nod, moving their separate ways about the small rooms. Kyle brought the girl to his bed, gently laying her down and tossing more blankets over her body. Strings of heat lanced up his arms and legs, burning his body. Freeing his hand, Kyle slowly pulled up one of sleeves, only faintly surprised when he saw the familiar curving black Marks taking shape on his body for the second time in several weeks.

Crouched beside the bed, he ran a gentle hand over her cheek, marveling at the soft skin. Her breathing had settled into a slow rhythm, no doubt resting in a deep sleep of dreams he couldn't begin to fathom. Small, vivid memories of those exact lips, curved in a knowing smile as she teased him, replayed in his mind. It was too sharp to not be a memory, yet he had never met her, only read of her in the paper the night they discovered her bed missing, a slipper on the roof. She was the Morgan girl, he knew it.

The sigh bubbled off his lips before he could think twice, and with a roll of the shoulders he rose. He should have known better; no matter how far he ran from the wild memories and visions plaguing his life, the quicker it found him. The girl before him was proof enough to that. Placing a finger on her cheek, the rush of memories swelled to life in his head again. Another, lovely memory rose the front of his mind, a song softer than downy wings on a baby duckling. He began to hum the tune, letting his lips subconsciously form the smile he'd been so desperately holding back.

Her eyes flung open.

He stepped back in haste, hands up defensively. The girl scrambled against the blankets and jacket, eyes wide and wild. But she didn't scream, didn't cry or shout. Instantly, he moved to soothe.

"Easy, calm down," he whispered hurriedly. Stealing a glance to make sure no one was watching them, he pressed his hands against her shoulders, keeping her steady. "Breathe."

She gasped for air, inhaling sharper than a knife cutting through skin. For a moment, Kyle wondered if she had ever taken a breath in her life, or if she was like a princess and his touch had awoken her from an everlasting slumber.

"What's your name?" He asked her.

Her eyes ran across the room, panic etched into the very corners of her bright, electric blue eyes. Even in her shocked state, he took her for a beauty. A fallen angel in the flesh, blessed to walk among the normal and fair.

Or maybe a curse.

Her mouth moved, a stutter of words colliding on her lips. "Where am I?" Her voice, soft and high, cracked on the last note. When Kyle didn't answer immediately, her next question came with a heightened fear. "Who are you?"

Without pressing further, he knew she wasn't playing. He made sure to keep his voice in check, soft and safe, like a lullaby. "It's going to be okay, we're going to take you home."

She appeared unconvinced, shaking her head with unmatched, terrified fury. Patches of pink stained her face, her skin hot to the touch. "No, I can't go back. He said I can't go back. They'll find me if I do."

"Who will find you?" He asked, pushing stray locks of the girl's tangled, wet blonde hair away from her face. His hand burned where their skin met. It was fever; the elements had gotten to her, after all. "Who is after you?"

Fingers touched the crook of the boy's elbow, and he jumped. The girl's hand had wrapped around his arm, her thin pianist like fingers softer than lamb's wool.

"Your skin... and your eyes..."

He looked down to where her half-lidded gaze rested, and froze. The Marks were back. He tilted his head to look back at her feverish eyes. The second they met, a small smile graced her lips, eyebrows rising high. Even in fever, she was curious.

Then the color in her eyes changed, knowledge and recognition flooding them with a strained panic.

"Kyle," she breathed, stunning him. He hadn't said his name, how did she know him? "He's back. He never died, Kyle, he's been waiting all along."

The words freed from his lips before he could think. "Lilix, it's okay. Who is after you?"

Pain shattered her beauty into tiny shards of dimly flickering hope. "I can't... I can't protect you. I have to protect you."

As soon as the words had left her lips, she closed her eyes, body collapsing into his arms. Kyle cursed under his breath, catching her. He pulled her tightly against his chest, cradling her and pressing his lips in a kiss on her head.

"Who are you trying to protect me from, my Ice

191

Princess?" He mumbled quietly. "Who is trying to break you?"
But no one would answer him.

AN ICE PRINCESS
HEART

ALIVIA ANDERS

RED ALICE PRESS

THE LOST AND DEAD

You can't drown your demons, once they know how to swim.

At first glance, the beach was enchanting. The skies looked painted, a collection of blue hues and fine clouds casting a glowing crown around the full moon. Sea green waves, cresting with a white and bubbling froth, crashed against the fine cream sand, rushing forward to the dry and exposed land.

Standing in the damp sand, Lilix Morgan could only see beauty. A gentle quiet cloaked the beach in a veil of secrecy, as if it were her private paradise tucked away from unwanted eyes. Her fingers brushed aside damp strands of blonde hair off her face, tucking it gently behind her ear. It seemed perfect, almost too perfect.

Could something really be too perfect?

The moment the thought struck through her subconscious, a souring pit of dread surfaced in her stomach. Her hand ran down the silken fabric of her white gown, frowning. She couldn't understand where the fear stemmed from, only that it carried a heavy premonition of promised and raw terror.

Moving to step back, Lilix watched as her paradise vanished before her eyes. Swaths of black consumed the sky until all that could be seen was a single beam of moonlight, shining on the ground before her feet. The ocean waters turned a deep red, pink froth flushing the sands to a dirty pink and brown. A bitter wind spun from the silence, whipping against her face no matter which way she turned.

Instinct told her to run, and she turned on her heels to head back for dry land. She stumbled, throwing out her hands to catch her fall, screaming as the sand hit her palms and knees. Sharp edges sliced into her skin, tiny cuts that bled as if she'd been stabbed all over her body. She quickly scrambled to her feet, fighting to ignore the bursts of pain exploding over her skin, when her toes brushed against something large and rough.

Every cell in her body shouted to run as fast as she could, but curiosity took hold. Shaking, Lilix looked down at the ground.

Bones, tens of hundreds of them, stood beneath her feet. They glistened white, damp with the red waters washing over them. Bile touched the back of her throat at the sight. Lilix pressed a hand to her mouth, shivering with fear. Her eyes roamed along the coastline, each passing glance instilling fear deep in her heart. As far as the eye could see, the sand had become a graveyard of bones in every which size and shape.

A rancid, nauseating smell choked the air, forcing Lilix to gag. Her eyes watered, and she searched about, only to shudder in even greater horror. Where the dolphins and seals once swam with the sea ran a line of connected bodies. They floated along the surface, torsos ripped open to expose their shredded, blackened insides.

Corpse-cold fingers wrapped around Lilix's throat from behind, a raspy voice hissing in her ear.

"This is what you get for taking from me what I loved the most," it said, laughing malevolently. "You will feel the same hopelessness I have, the same desperation mirroring my tainted soul."

"Who are you?" Lilix whispered, frozen to the ground. A chill stirred in her chest, her power willing to surface, but no ice gathered on her fingertips. "What do you want from me?"

All at once, the sounds of the beach cut out, leaving only the rattling breath of her tormentor to fill her ears.

"I want your heart."

TWELVE STOLEN SOULS

Crammed in the petite kitchen of a cottage just outside a beach town in France, Prisitus Mallow stared hollowly at the wall across the room. "It's nearly sunrise," she said, fingers quivering as she wrapped strands of her caramel colored hair around dainty fingers. She eyed each of the other three girls with her in numb shock. "She still isn't back."

"Have patience," Estrella mumbled for the hundredth time, bristling slightly. Where Prisitus fretted and fidgeted in her seat, Estrella maintained a carefully crafted persona of calm. "She'll return soon, I'm sure of it."

Pris glared sharper than daggers. "Are you claiming Sight now, dear sister?"

"Not in the least."

"Then I suggest you hold your tongue. You don't know what I know."

Nestled deep in the farthest corner of the kitchen, another one of the girls spoke up. Tinges of bold, orange flame danced on her fingertips as she held her hand out, poised as if a wine glass were nestled there.

"For the Composer's sake Pris, just tell us what you saw and cut the bloody dramatics," the girl in the corner snapped, her crimson dress shifting as she stepped closer to the wooden table. Straight, sleek raven colored hair washed over her bare shoulders. The dresses of the time period were a far cry from the tunics and robes they'd grown accustomed to covering their necklines. "Unless this is simply another petty attempt at seeking attention."

Prisitus ignored her, as she had all night. Her hands continued to twist hair around her fingers, weaving in and out to the rhythm of nerves clustering in her stomach. It had started as an uneasy feeling, as if the ground beneath her were slipping away. She knew the sensation well; first came the slipping sensation, followed by a lightheaded wave. By the time the world bled to black, she knew the Sight was at hand, ripping her forward in time and showing her the fragile, destructive future of someone close.

Standing up, Prisitus made for the door, only to stop at the frame and stare at the silent body blocking the way. A gown of soft lilac decorated the girl like a doll of fine china, tiny white flowers woven in her tightly clustered black curls running nearly to her knees.

"Kathryn, please," Prisitus pled, voice cracking. "She's in danger, I can feel it. Tell Arabella we need to leave. We need to find her before it's too late."

The girl in purple, Kathryn, turned her eyes to the girl in red. "Ara, we should go."

"No." Arabella snapped, shaking her head. Hues of red colored her dark eyes as she narrowed them. "We don't need to do anything until Pris stops acting like this, and tells us what she saw."

Stepping back, Pris placed a hand against her temple. Her

breath catching in her chest, she tried to force down the waves of memory from her vision. Sandy shores, washed in a fresh bath of blood, painted a grim picture in her head. Had Lilix been there, she wouldn't have questioned Pris's cry. She knew how the visions worked, how dark and catastrophically true they became. A moment of Sight was like a poison-tipped knife; while the knife appeared to be the lethal weapon, it was only a red herring to mask the real threat that promised death.

She moved back to the table, staring at the swirling pattern carefully etched into the wood. She could feel the weight of their stares drilling into her from all directions. They all were waiting for her to give up the words trapped in her heart, the fear that one of them was missing.

Sighing, Pris forced the words from her mouth, but not before she stole a glance at Arabella's glowering stare. "It was a vision of Lilix." It wasn't the first time Pris had seen the youngest of their group in danger. Judging by the way Lilix was known to handle things, it wouldn't be the last, either.

Behind her, Katie stiffened. One word tore from her lips. "Where?"

Pris opened her mouth to speak, only to go quiet. Tiny, mint green leaves sprouted from her fingers and palms. Her green eyes swept over to the door, watching as it inched open and a figure stepped in. All four girls went silent.

Bathed in a sea of red stains and salt water on her pure white gown, Lilix stood in the doorway. Mixtures of sticky, dark red blood speckled her skin. As she crossed the room, bloody footprint trailed behind.

"The beach," Lilix cut in with a wicked grin, studying each face as she took in the mixture of indifferent and horrified expressions at her appearance. This marked the fifth time this month she'd come home unannounced, dressed in blood like a butcher fresh from the slaughter, but only Pris knew. Exchanging glances with the emerald-eyed prophet,

Lilix's grin widened. "Pris had seen me at the beach."

The silence barely lasted two heartbeats before Katie launched forward, took Lilix by the shoulders, and violently shook her. *"What did you do?"*

She waited for the shaking to subside before stepping free from Katie's lingering grasp. She sighed loudly. "Relax, it's not my blood."

A disgusted look marred Katie's face. She grabbed a fistful of fabric, turning the stained folds of Lilix's dress back and forth. Inwardly, guilt struck at her like a lightning encrusted harpoon. Katie had worried for her, she had put together that much by the dark spiral of violet clouds covering the shoreline, swallowing the rising sun. Had it been a normal day, Lilix would have chided her best friend for letting her emotions pool into the magic they so carefully guarded in the veins.

"Then, whose blood is it?"

Lilix turned her gaze to the source of the question, slipping an innocent look of neutrality over her features. "Honestly, I have no clue. I don't quite remember getting to the beach."

Eyes narrowed to slits, Arabella pointed a finger at the blood covered blonde. "I think you're lying."

"Then why don't you tell us?" Lilix smiled, sweet like a lion approaching its freshly killed prey. "If you think you presume to know the truth."

A hiss slipped between her lips. Arabella swore under her breath. Gathering her skirts, she weaved through the room until her feet toed Lilix's.

"You may be the Composer's chosen leader of us all, but I am done following you. Watch your back," she snapped, fire kindling in her eyes as she bent closer. Orange tipped the hairs on her skin, as if she were a single flame burning to life. "Or you might forfeit that pretty little crown."

She swept from the room in a brush of fabric and fire, leaving the other four to their devices. After several minutes, Rea joined her, followed by Katie as she mumbled over the pity of Lilix's ruined dress. Streaks of golden yellow sunlight sliced through the thin curtains covering the large window encasing the back of the room, bathing the remaining two in a pure, buttercup glow.

Pris eyed her, traces of sorrow shadowing her earth-toned features. Since the Composer's creation of them all, Lilix had found each carried an ethereal beauty no mortal could ever hope to match. Over the years, their perfect skin, striking eyes, and melodic voices brought attention of all sorts, some good, most not. It was how they ended up here, living in a tiny town on the edge of their first home many centuries ago, secluded from civilization, yet close enough to join them and appear normal.

Studying some of the stains on her dress, Lilix brushed a hand over the fabric. One by one, the stains, dirt, and smell of sea water vanished. "Well, this complicates things."

"I'm sorry," Pris said quietly. "I had no choice but to wake them all."

Dress clean, Lilix moved her hand over the table, watching with vague interest as a dusting of frost created a glossy sheen on top the wood.

"Did you?" Lilix questioned softly.

"You were gone too long this time." Nervously, Pris shot a look over her shoulders before continuing. "I... I didn't know what to do. How was I supposed to know you would come home safe and not some pile of flesh and bone at the bottom of the sea?"

"Pris," Lilix kindly patted her on the shoulder. "We can't die, remember?"

"That doesn't mean you can't be hurt," Pris went on, the words tumbling from her mouth like a waterfall. "The visions are getting worse. Whatever it is you're chasing, it knows, and if it gets the chance, it will do you harm."

Coming from a prophet, the words should have instilled a chill deep in Lilix's heart. But it was hard to fear anything when death evaded you, hard to feel the cold grip of terror when you were an ice princess who could wield shards of ice like throwing knives.

Instead, it only fueled her need to solve the mystery plaguing the towns along the coast. In less than four months, twelve stolen souls joined the sea of the dead in ways no person, mortal or immortal, should ever see. Let alone endure.

Reaching out, Pris held onto one of Lilix's hands. White ice and green leaves met, tipping them in a delicate frost.

"I'm worried," she confessed, a pinch of blush tinting her warm cheeks. "What if this... this killer can end you? What will become of us?"

Lilix shifted, skirts swishing with the sudden turn. Her free hand cupped Pris's cheek gently.

"It isn't going to happen, I promise. The visions are getting worse because whoever is murdering these innocent souls knows it's close to being caught." She smiled with a mixture of mischief and excitement. "I will find the source of the deaths, and together we will end them."

A FROSTED BABY BLUE

The trip in town was only supposed to take an hour or two, yet five hours later, and Katie was no closer to dragging Pris and Lilix home.

Wandering aimlessly along the lane of tiny shops, Pris twirled in her periwinkle gown of silk satin. Tiny flowers were woven into her high-piled, curling hair.

Lilix stared at the fistful of field flowers she held with a twinkle in her eye. She sniffed each one before sighing in content. "I think the only thing that's never bothered me about the sea, is that everything around it smells like salt water and fresh earth."

"Not even *un petit peu?*" Pris grinned, glancing over her shoulder back at the blonde. Lilix shook her head, smiling.

Further back, Katie sighed heavily. She shifted the basket from one arm to the next, taking hold of her purple gown to avoid a mud puddle. "Can we leave now? We'll have no time for songs tonight if we don't move faster."

Ignoring, Lilix paid little attention to the protest. She knew that Katie's complaint was valid, and they really should have made their way home by now to prep for songs with the Composer. But the ice princess had another thing in mind, one that involved a little less tension and much more embarrassment.

Skirt held up, Lilix dashed to Pris's side and dropped her skirts to take hold of the girl's shoulders. Before them the town opened wide, populated streets filled from side to side as people traveled between shops for clothes and other assorted items. In the center stood a cream fountain, etched with artwork most crafters could only dream of creating.

"Pris, look!" Lilix pointed toward the fountain, grinning. "Isn't that *Monsieur Jerret?*"

At once Pris went still, frozen to the ground. A mask of horror and awe widened her emerald eyes, and she gasped.

"No, no no no no no!" She turned to Lilix and hunched into the folds of her dress. "Please, we must leave. Jerret can't see me like this!"

Katie giggled from behind the two, head shaking. "See you how? As a beautiful and very available woman? Or as a coward huddled in someone else's dress, hiding like a child?"

As she said it, Pris stood straight as a plank. Between the color drained from her face and the blush on her cheeks, she almost looked comical. Her eyes never strayed from the slender figure standing near the fountain, dressed in a simple suit and coat, his dark brown hair hidden under a top hat. Lilix didn't understand the infatuation Pris carried for the man, only that it was unlike anything she'd ever felt before. The idea that her True could be such a simple, lackluster French man nearly made Lilix laugh. Wasn't love, and the discovery of one's True, supposed to be with a magical being that made your heart sing?

"Just look at him, he has the most beautiful eyes." Pris

giggled, and Lilix gave her a confused stare. She pointed at the blonde's eyes. "Kind of like yours, a frosted blue shielding the summer sun. Did you ever notice the small ring of gold around your pupil?"

"I'm sure she doesn't spend *that* much in front of a mirror," Katie said, rolling her eyes to the heavens. She changed subjects, returning to Pris. "Does he really make you feel that special?"

At the question, a dreamy, faraway look passed over Pris's face. Lilix could only begin to wonder what sort of imagination the girl had when it came to Jerret and his quiet demeanor. Perhaps that was his appeal- that he said so little to keep every girl hooked on the few words that did grace his lips.

Grasping for words, Pris plucked a flower from the bunch in Lilix's hand, and stepped off to the side. She twisted and twirled the tiny green stem between her fingertips. "It's like, I forget how to breathe when I think of him. Like the sun could never stop shining if he stayed close. I look at him and see my heart."

Katie and Lilix exchanged confused, and equally pensive looks. Neither one had ever come close to finding one to call their True, and not for lack of trying. The Composer had made it clear that to each one of them was a match, a second half of their souls, waiting to be found when the time is right. Tens of thousands years later, and Lilix was starting to think there would be no hope of ever finding her other half.

A True was one who completed you, one who made you stronger both inside and out. Out of the five, Arabella had been the first to find her True. He had been bold, strong, and carried a fiery temper just as volatile as hers. Together, they balanced each other in a way that hadn't been seen before. All seemed well, until the unthinkable happened, and Arabella made the biggest mistake possible.

As if reading her mind, Katie leaned closer, whispering. "Do you think we'll ever find ours?"

She wondered the same thing, day in and out. Lilix tried not to sound heartbroken, in case Pris could hear.

"Truth be told, every day that passes with no luck leaves me with a bitter taste." She bit her lower lip. "I'm starting to think maybe my True will never find me, or I find them."

Katie's forehead wrinkled. "Do you really believe that?" When Lilix nodded, she sighed. "Lilix, we'll all have our chance. You will find the one that your heart sings for. The Composer promised."

"And what if he was wrong?" She shot back, not meaning to sound brash. "What if not finding my True is punishment for the cruel choice I had to make against Arabella?"

Katie gasped, causing Pris to turn around. Both girls blanched, appearing visibly uncomfortable. Eyes trained on the ground, Lilix tried to ignore the obvious stares. Mentioning that tragic night was forbidden ground, one that each girl avoided to skirt around the greater issue; that one of their own had gone against the rules bonded into their blood.

Trying to soothe, Katie reached out a hand. "Lilix-"

She brushed the contact away, pinching her eyes shut. Hot tears beaded in the corners of her eyes. "No, please, I don't deserve comfort or pity."

"Arabella made her choice. She broke the rules, not you," Pris said, quivering. Quietly, she added, "You did what had to be done."

Forcing her eyes open, Lilix snapped. "Did I? Did I really have to let her only love for all of eternity die like that? She'll never forgive me, she can barely stand to be in the same room with me, let alone hold a conversation outside of double-ended sentences promising threats and attacks."

In a single move, Katie shuffled forward and wrapped her arms around the sniffling girl. She kissed both her cheeks.

"She'll forgive you, in time. One day she will see the mistake she made by cutting you out of her heart." She dabbed her fingertips against the corners of Lilix's eyes, brushing away the pooling tears. "Come on now, let's head back home."

"Wait." Lilix glanced over at Pris. She gave a weak smile. "Do me a favor? Don't panic, but a certain someone is coming right this way."

Pris opened her mouth to object, and turned around to see a familiar pile of dark brown hair hiding under a top hat. Smiling, Jerret held out his hand for hers in true gentleman fashion. "*Madam Mallow*, keeping well on this fine day I hope?"

She held out her hand, red bruising her flushed cheeks when his lips descended on the skin. A cluster of words tumbled from her mouth, nothing coherent.

He grinned, the glimmer of intrigue sparking in his gaze. "Perhaps I shall see you again, say tomorrow at this very spot?"

Pris nodded with a jerk of the head, eyes wider than the moon. "*Oui*, I would be honored."

"It's a date." He kissed her hand once more, only this time he let his lips linger for a moment longer than needed. His eyes never left hers. "I eagerly await the moon to fall from the sky, so I know it will be time to find you once more."

They both bid each other a good day, and Jerret walked down beyond the water fountain before vanishing altogether. For a moment, neither girl moved. Katie and Lilix kept their eyes trained on Pris. She stood there, stunned into silence, hand hanging midair as if held by an invisible impression of Jerret.

Then, very slowly, Pris moved the hand to cradle it against her chest. "Have mercy on my soul, my blue eyed angel."

MONSTER IN DISGUISE

Later that night, the whispers began.

Lilix had barely drifted to sleep when the melody began to float through her mind, spinning pictures of a world where she hadn't harmed those she loved the most. A world where there was no need to worry over danger at every corner for using her magic, a place she ached to call home. The night stirred tiny drifts of wind against her cheek as they floated through the open window at the foot of her bed.

"Come to me, Lilix. We must speak privately."

As if animated by strings, her body rose. Each arm hung weakly by her side. Quietly as she could, the entranced blonde slipped out of her window, and made for the sea cliffs north of their cottage house.

Rough, knee-high sea grass scratched and tugged on the hem of her white nightgown as she lurched forward, one jerky movement after the next. Lilix stirred, opening her eyes just as her limbs gave another awkward twitch closer to the sea cliff. She could make out the roar of ocean waters crashing against the craggy rock below.

Immediately she cried out, and flung herself backwards into the ground. The invisible pull instantly vanished, and she collapsed into the tall grass. Shock and horror and adrenaline coursed through her like an electric shock, her mind a mess. How had she gotten here? Who was leading her to the first place she ever saw when she was created?

A head came into view above, hiding the moon and creating a dark mask over his face. "Trouble in paradise, Lilix?"

Oh hell!

Lilix scrambled up to her feet and jumped back immediately. Under the beams of silken moonlight, the Composer appeared regal in his crimson robe and gold detailing of Marks. Long waves of dirty blonde hair framed his sharp face, creating deep hollow pools around his glowing, crystal blue eyes.

Instantly, she swore, kicking at the ground. Frost collected on her eyelids and cheekbones as she glared up to the Composer. "You? You're the reason I've been waking up in places, covered in blood?"

He shook his head immediately, eyes bright. "No, this is the first time I've called for you."

So there was something still after her, something dark and itching to fulfill its bloodlust. Lilix pressed the thought of an unknown enemy aside, and studied the Composer carefully.

"Why call only me?" Hesitantly, she asked. "Why not wait until our songs tomorrow?"

Meeting his eyes, it was then that she noticed the sorrow in his stare, the grief and agony that was tearing him apart on the inside. Normally the Composer would smile, even play a game of riddles with hidden lessons if the day called for it.

Sorrow wasn't in the Composer's demeanor, wasn't something he'd ever show willingly to his creations unless it was required.

"What's going on?" Lilix fearfully asked, echoing her still unanswered questions. She took a step back. "Why did you call me?"

Swallowing, he ran a hand through his long locks. "What I am about to tell you, you must listen to carefully. It's too late for the mortal, but I can spare you and the others before this happens again."

"Before what happens?" She felt her eyes grow wide, breath quickening. "What mortal?"

Inch by inch, he turned his back to her, staring out at the midnight sea. Bursts of starlight made it look as if diamonds swam in the rocky waves away from shore.

"One of you has spent more time with a mortal recently," he said slowly, then paused. "I'm afraid his life had already been ripped from its protective shell."

The words acted like a fiery punch to the gut. Jerret was the only mortal they had prolonged contact with as of late. Which meant... he was dead. Pris's heart wouldn't survive the truth.

Trying to digest the news proved harder than she cared to admit. She blinked, fighting the wave of tears that threatened to provoke a bitter rage. In a low breath, she asked, "Was he murdered, like the rest of them?"

Silently, the Composer nodded.

Pain pulsed in her chest. She placed both hands against her face, covering her eyes as she fought to keep herself calm. If Pris had truly felt something for that boy, he could have been her True. With him dead, she'd never know what true love was, never experience it in her endless lifetime. Even if he was not hers, his death was not warranted.

Fists clenched and teeth bared, Lilix growled. "What is killing these people, Composer? What is slaughtering the town?"

"Have you not seen it?"

"No," she shook her head vigorously. "Every time I come to the beach and find another body, it's too late. Only the ghost of its presence torments me, and tells me it wants my heart."

The Composer was in front of her before she could blink, hands pressed against her face. He locked eyes with her, stealing a deep breath before speaking the words that would chill her more than her own power.

"You know who is slaughtering the innocent."

She felt her knees go weak, but held herself upright as best she could. "H-how well?"

"As well as you know yourself."

She screamed in denial, shoving back from the Composer hard enough for him to fall on his back. Ice lanced from the ground in a dance of deadly spikes. "No! It can't be one of the others! They know how valuable life is to us!"

Steadily, he rose. "The one you seek is a wolf, Lilix. A wolf in sheep's clothing. A wolf whose mate was slaughtered by the shepherd, and in turn slaughtered the shepherd's herd." He leaned forward on the balls of his feet, tensing as two spikes of ice shot up and scraped his cheeks. "Do you understand what I am telling you?"

Lilix raised an frost-tipped finger, pointing accusingly. "You lie. She wouldn't dare."

"She would. After her beloved was ended by your hand."

The rage she had tried to keep contained flowed over. Her blonde hair whipped about as ice crystalized on her hands, protective white Marks raising up on her skin.

"I did what I had to- she broke the one rule that cannot be broken, you told us that the day we were created." A deep hum vibrated in the air, chaotic strings of music erratically rising and falling in volume. Her eyes glowed bright as stars.

"Do not tell me I acted in the wrong."

Hands raised, the Composer gently shook his head. "You didn't. You did exactly as I had instructed you to."

Praise was not what she needed to continue harnessing her wild energy. Her eyes flickered, wavering. "Then what are you telling me?"

"That you must confront her, Lilix. You must stop her before another innocent life is taken."

If she understood, then what he was suggesting...

"And how do you suggest I go about that?" She asked, raising her eyebrows in surprise when the Composer merely grinned.

"Easy," he said. "You must unmask the wolf."

"Where have you been?"

Hours later, Pris's voice cut through the burning sunrise as Lilix walked back. Hues of orange and yellow danced in the sky, a welcoming sight of happiness that would soon look like a grim reminder when each morning would come, and Pris would be without her possible love.

"Pris, get the others," Lilix said, bypassing the stunned girl and making for the kitchen. She normally would stop and stare, even admire the few pieces of artwork decorating the walls, but not today. Not with the words she had prepared on her tongue.

Slowly, each of them rose from their beds and joined Lilix in the kitchen. No one spoke of her disheveled appearance, of her torn nightgown and grass stains.

And after she spoke the words, no one would care. "Pris, Jerret is dead."

The words acted like a pistol, locked and loaded. The happy, yet uncertain girl went from stunned and horrified, to violent and defiant. Tears welled in her eyes and she screamed, raw and unforgiving, as vines erupted through the cottage walls and entwined along the objects in the room, suffocating them. Rea moved at once, leaping for her sister and embracing her in an iron grasp.

"Pris, calm down!" She cried.

"No!" She screeched, kicking violently against Rea's struggling grasp. "He's not, you lie, stop lying!"

It suddenly turned quiet, save for the voice of one who snickered in disbelief.

"You're crying over a mortal? Oh, boo hoo, Pris, grow up. There's plenty more where that came from," Arabella rolled her eyes, waiving a hand dismissively.

Pris hissed. "You know nothing, shut it."

"Oh, I know nothing? They're animals," Arabella sneered, flicking a strand of hair behind her shoulder. "One step above mindless, carnivorous beasts that roam on land. Who are we to interfere with their bizarre habits of mindlessly slaughtering each other for sport?"

"This kind of murder is not for sport!" Lilix roared, slamming her hands on the table hard enough to make the plates jump. Frost covered her fingers. "This is someone enacting revenge, or a killer with an intense hatred for men. And it's using dark magic to do it."

Across the table, Katie covered her mouth and gasped. The room had gone still, frozen in a breath of time as Lilix's words hung in the air like smoke. Until this point, she hadn't mentioned a single thing about the murders. Opening the door the revelation that another magical being, human or otherwise, was assisting in murders, carried the weight of a thousand deaths.

Very slowly, Katie lowered her mouth. "You... you're sure of this?"

Lilix nodded, never taking her eyes off Arabella as she blanched.

"I am, and I intend to stop whoever it is."

ALL IS ASHES AND DUST

Two weeks later.

The tiny pub on Main reeked, more so than the last twelve nights passed. Swells of smoke, fog thicker than pea soup, and the rotting stench hovering over the Thames painted a vulgar, nauseating taste on the tongue that neither food nor alcohol could shake. Any soul of pure heart or sound mind would never step foot into the wild and untamed night.

But there were those few, the eclectic bizarre who took the forbidding night not as a worry, but as a challenge. Those who dared to venture out into the rancid night for the personal comfort only a mug of mead could bring. That, or a leg of a fine lady willing to offer a private service. Word had it that if one sought both brew and bust, Porter's on Main was the place to go.

Of course, that was assuming you wanted to be seen in such a place.

For a Friday night, the pub was unnaturally silent. Waves of crime and superstition had pushed patrons home, leaving the bold few to enter for their nightly fix. Against the farthest corner of the rotting pub, two bodies sat close, a blend of legs and arms under swaths of mauve and black fabric. The sound of lips against skin brought a shivered giggle to sound, the sigh of a female as she tossed her loose, raven black hair over her shoulder.

"You make the most beautiful sounds," said the male, continuing to kiss her again, his lips pressing against the inside of her wrist hungrily. "It is but fine music to my ears."

The raven-haired beauty giggled once more, this time deep and smooth. "It has been said I can bring an entire orchestra to their knees with the sounds I make." She inched closer to the male, hovering her lips inches from the skin on his neck. "Perhaps you'll be fortunate enough to hear all the sounds I am capable of making."

Together the pair meshed, too enveloped in their wicked desires to notice the lone woman sitting nearby. Her dark blue gown blended expertly within the shadows, a wide-brimmed velvet hat encasing the bright blonde hair resting under the cap. With pursed lips she watched the couple rise from their seats, the woman casting a quick glance about the room before pinning her dark hair into an unkempt bun, and leaving with the male.

A sigh slipping off her lips, Lilix stood from her half-hidden seat, and made sure to follow. The couple didn't need to go far; vacant rooms left for use were only up a flight of steps and down a single, narrow hall. As Lilix trailed after the couple, she could only shudder as she took in the sight of the seedy, flickering lights and peeling, stained wallpaper. Grateful sleeves adorned her arms so her skin wouldn't make contact with the walls, she cautiously pressed herself against the wall outside the door at the end of the hall, straining to hear the

215

voices inside.

Groans from the male grew louder, the sound of fabric shoved aside as skirt fabric came undone. Before she could stop herself, Lilix spun into the room, flinging the door open with surprising strength.

The raven-haired girl froze, her petite form mounted above the burly man beneath her. Her hair had come undone once more, silken locks of inky black tresses cascading over her shoulders and arms, fanning out like a coat over her mauve colored dress.

Flipping her hair away from her face, the burlesque beauty spoke. "Good to know I'm being followed now by the pretentious ethereal one."

Lilix made for the bed, grabbing an arm and pulling the girl off the male. Surprisingly, he made no move, but only stared at the ceiling with vacant eyes, a cloud of white covering the iris.

"What in the Composer's name is wrong with you, Arabella?" Lilix hissed in a pitiful attempt to sound intimidating. "So this is what you've been doing, where you've been going, after our songs?"

Arabella jerked her arm free from the blonde's feeble grasp. Her eyes burned, flames flickering within the bleeding red circling her pupils. "What I do in my spare time is none of your business."

"The hell it is," Lilix said in a snap, reaching for Arabella's sleeveless arm once more. She instantly took notice of how her Marks had grown darker, different shades of grey instead of the pristine white the rest of them had. Soon, they would be black, and then what? "Twelve men, Arabella. Twelve mortal souls have been ripped from this world, from this town, thirteen if you count Jerret. The townsfolk are terrified to leave their own homes. Tell me you aren't the one they're after, tell me it isn't you doing this."

The raven-haired girl came closer, leaving little space between their faces. "Get out." Her growl rattled her voice, the sound raising goose bumps on Lilix's skin. "This is none of your concern."

For a moment, neither of them moved, only the sound of their breathing breaking the silence dancing between them. After a minute, Arabella moved back, turning to the dazed man on the bed. A low, sultry purr sounded in her throat, and she moved up along his legs, bringing herself to rest just above his hips.

"I know what this is about," Lilix softly challenged. Arabella said nothing. The words whispered off her lips, a wisp of words. "He wouldn't have wanted this, Ara."

Arabella paused, her wandering hands at a stand still. "And what," she said, tone low and threatening. "Would you claim to know about what he wanted?"

It was the last straw on the camel's back. Ice surged in her veins, malice coating her tongue thick. "Oh come on, you really think he would have thought this was okay? You really think he would have enjoyed watching you spread your legs for any male that looked at you twice?"

The black-haired temptress was off the bed and in front of Lilix faster than she could blink. Her hand whipped, smacking Lilix hard enough to send a mortal hurtling into the wall.

"Say it again, ice wench."

Challenge presented, Lilix closed the gap between both of them. Frost coated her fingertips as the temperature within the room dropped to a bitter winter. Her eyes, normally a light heavenly blue, glowed with an electric pulse.

"He wouldn't have wanted this," she repeated with force.

"Don't presume to know what he wanted, he's dead!"

"And who's fault is that?" Lilix sneered, frost up to her elbows. Thin, white Marks rose from her skin like a submerged tattoo, a collage of lines and notes painted on her as if she were a sheet of music paper. "Don't play coy and put this on me, Arabella Haven. You knew that by taking another man after being bound to your True would break the Marks, you knew it would taint you and kill him."

"You could have saved him!" She screamed, wild with grief. "You have the power, you could have saved him from his suffering. Instead, you chose to use me as a example, and my only love is dead because of you." Marks surfaced on her skin, spreading across her neck and down her shoulders. "And now, because of you, no one in our precious little group will have happiness and love. For as long as I continue to exist, bound to this world and realm as the Composer's puppet and bearing the scarlet letter you've branded me with, I will make sure none of you find happiness."

Frost lanced free from Lilix's palm and she grasped it, shaping it to a thick dagger of ice.

"I would be very, very careful in what you say next," she warned with a deadly glare in her icy eyes.

Arabella wasted no time. "You and the others will never know what true love is, I swear on it."

ALIVIA ANDERS is the author of the bestselling Illumine Series. Born and raised in PA, she fell headfirst into the world of writing at thirteen with the discovery of internet fan-fiction and RPG-forum boards. A lover of chinchillas, mexican food, and coffee, she spends most of her time drumming up new ideas to spin into tales to enchant readers everywhere.

www.ingramcontent.com/pod-product-compliance
Lightning Source LLC
Chambersburg PA
CBHW021137130626
46554CB00005B/1552